Flicking Boogers
in the Wind

Jonathan Bricklin

Author's Note

All the nouns in this story are of course fictions and fabrications, almost goes without saying. Any resemblance to actual people or places or things is entirely coincidental. Nevertheless, all the verbs and especially the adjectives are true.

Flicking boogers in the wind is pretty darn inconsiderate, not to mention illegal.

-Alabama Highway Patrol

The real secret is that the world is made up of words. And if you know the words that the world is made of, you can make of it whatever you wish.

-Terrence McKenna

Flicking Boogers in the Wind

Prologue

Lake Titicaca is nestled high in the Andes Mountains between Peru and Bolivia. It's filled to the brim with mysterious oddities. Renowned underwater explorer Jacques Cousteau went on an expedition there one time in 1969, searching for a legendary, fire-breathing, people-eating, snot-bubble-blowing amphibious dragon that was nowhere to be seen.

What Captain Cousteau found instead was tens of thousands of purple and green and tangerine *Telmatobius* water frogs hiding on the bottom of the lake in complete silence. Not a ribbit. After further investigation it became clear that these frogs had magnificently large scrotums and pensive, bordering on taciturn, personalities. It turned out that they were simply scared stiff and lying low, afraid of being eaten alive by the Uros, an ancient tribe of pre-Incan Floating Island people with a penchant for frog legs.

Call it bad luck, perhaps, but the frogs are victims of proximity. The Uros live directly above them on a cluster of miniature islands the size of suburban blocks, woven together from mud and straw and peat and reeds and a lot of hard work, anchored to the lake bed with ropes and rocks and twigs, and requiring endless maintenance.

The concept of time doesn't exist for the Uros. They don't wear watches or pay taxes, and they're never late for an appointment. They don't even have electricity or indoor plumbing; needless to say the Internet is nowhere to be found. They have no modern conveniences, yet they've managed to float along just fine for thousands of years. The Uros rely on ancient medicine, mystical sorcery, and dramatic storytelling to compensate for their lack of modern amenities. There is no government and no official law, just guidelines, common courtesy, and hierarchy. They keep it simple. They don't steal, because they'll get caught. They don't lie, because there's no point. And they're not lazy, because they'll drown.

Miguel Battabooshka Guadeloupe Garcia-Rodriguez is an award-winning break-dancer, Pulitzer Prize-winning poet, part-time sword and fire swallower, and full-time magical shaman. He's a hero to the Uros, much like David Blaine is to the Americans. A shaman is a messenger between the human and the spirit worlds, similar to a witch, without the cackle or broom or bad rap.

Shamans are required to wear a number of different hats each day, including: acting as the village's spiritual advisor, like a priest or a rabbi or a TV evangelist; mixing potions and casting magic spells, like a doctor or pharmacist; and predicting the future, like the weatherman or a Magic 8-Ball or Warren Buffett.

Oftentimes shamans require the assistance of plants and animals to perform their conjuring. These function as conduits between the super and the natural, the yin and the yang, the boom and the bang. Snakes and turtles and crocodiles are the most common collaborators with shamans; turtles in particular are the cat's pajamas as far as reptilian sorcery is concerned, probably because of their ancient wisdom and easygoing temperament, in comparison to crocodiles.

Miguel's most cherished colleague was a very old and rare mata mata turtle named Marvilloso the Mythical IV. Marvilloso was grayish brown and oblong and small for his species, about five inches from stem to stern. But he had a big personality, he was gregarious and hilarious, and he could karaoke in four languages (Spanish, Portuguese, Cantonese, and English). His shell was bulletproof and waterproof and SPF-1000-proof, which played a part in preserving his youthful appearance. He didn't look a day over one century, despite having lived nearly two.

Each evening after dinner, dessert, and espresso, Marvilloso would drift to sleep in the warmer shallow water of the lake, floating on his back under the twinkling stars, not a care in the world. In the morning, after sunrise, he would wipe the sleep from his eyes and stretch the retractable vertebrae of his neck. Then he'd swallow a naive little fish in one big bite. "What a waste of time chewing is," he often mused while patting his belly. After that he'd floss with seaweed and gargle with lake water and waddle his way to his job as a shaman's executive assistant.

Waddling was a way of life for a turtle. The exact way in which you waddled, with a swagger or a strut, with emphasis or not, was a very important decision, and played a large part in how the village people perceived you. Marvilloso understood this all too well, and had spent the better half of his first century refining his waddle, never complacent, never satisfied, always trying to improve, constantly experimenting with new rhythms and styles and attitudes, and even once inventing a gravity-defying reverse foot-slide that Michael Jackson, a childhood break-dancing friend of Miguel's and a frequent visitor to the village in the early 1970s, would later master and call the Moonwalk.

Once Marvilloso was safely aboard Miguel's island and inside his roofless straw hut, they would begin the day by sipping cappuccinos brewed over a fire, followed by deep meditation for fifteen minutes, sometimes twenty, depending on the current state of village affairs. Meditation was followed immediately by a thirty-minute, high-impact, intense and invigorating watercolor painting session designed to express their deepest and most unconscious thoughts and ideas.

After painting they'd stretch and do a few downward dogs, followed by a kata (an aikido training session) for forty-five minutes to an hour. Aikido is the art of unifying with life's energy, and Marvilloso was extraordinarily good at it (especially for a reptile), the best, some say, since Morihei Ueshiba, who created aikido as an expression of his personal philosophy of universal peace and reconciliation. After aikido Miguel and Marvilloso usually split an appetizer portion of high-protein chocolate-covered grasshoppers, downed a few iced cappuccinos, and went back to the work of telepathically decoding the harmonic particle waves of the universe, and then rearranging the molecular impurities passing through the village.

Telepathy is like Bluetooth for your brain, bypassing the mouth, tongue, lips, and vocal cords to communicate directly between minds. Everyone's capable of thinking and communicating telepathically, even without signing a long-term service plan, but unlike Verizon or AT&T, telepathy is a delicate art form that must be studied. Like most languages, it's difficult to learn after a certain age, and virtually impossible when you're all grown up and your brain synapses have been super-glued shut.

To watch Miguel and Marvilloso engaging in their nonverbal but volatile and impassioned conversations, rapid-fire, back and forth, like sports commentators calling a game without moving their lips or making a sound, was disconcerting yet mesmerizing. Miguel did the color commentary (details and descriptions), and Marvilloso did the play-by-play (who, what, when, where, why), not about basketball, of course, but about plants and animals and politics and other ethereal things.

In the afternoon they swam to shore to collect the flowers and plants required for the magic potions of the day. These they brewed in a copper caldron hung above a roaring fire in the middle of Miguel's roofless hut. Sitting Indian-style, eyes closed and holding hands, Miguel and Marvilloso would chant rap songs from the nineties while the magical brew bubbled before them. The hut would shake, rattle, and roll, the ground would sway, the lake would ripple, and the village people would smile, knowing they were in good hands.

The buying and selling of exotic animals is big business on Planet Earth. The rarer the better, and as an animal approaches total extinction its price goes through the roof, making psychopathic animal poachers delirious with greed and willing to do almost anything to get their dirty hands on one.

Some people enjoy shark's fin soup, others prefer penguin livers or dolphin brains, but sadly turtle soup is by far the most popular these days. For which we have William Howard Taft to thank. The twenty-seventh president of the United States was a fanatic for turtle soup, an unabashed, unrepentant, complete and total nut for it. And in the sweltering summer months when it was too hot for soup, the President slurped mint turtle gelato smoothies like they were going out of style.

Sometimes Miguel would have an unexplained rumbling feeling in the center of his belly, similar to indigestion, but regarding the safety of his friend and colleague. At any time a mata mata turtle like Marvilloso could fall victim to the worldwide turtle soup craze, or could sell for a thousand dollars or more in a classy pet store because of his rarity and age and winning personality.

Early one morning as the sun rose over Lake Titicaca, shades of orange and red and purple danced across the glass water, and for a split second all was right with the world, epic tranquility as far as the eye could see. Then the moment passed and apocalyptic black raspberry clouds rolled in fast.

Faintly at first, like the purring of a hyena, the rhythmic swooshing of helicopter blades spilled over the mountaintops, followed by a fleet of ultramodern military planes dually equipped with helicopter blades on the wings. They peeked their malevolent noses down at the lake, their fuselages resembling pelican beaks with capacious pouches presumably designed for swooping up turtles.

They flew fast and dove low. They seemed angry as they skimmed the water's surface and dropped their hatch doors to release sprawling nets that corralled everything in their path. Including Marvilloso, who found himself trapped in a turtle tank in a pet store in the middle of nowhere before he realized which way was up.

How could it be that an all-knowing and powerful magical turtle like Marvilloso, who could predict the future, cure incurable diseases, paint, sing, dance, and do the Moonwalk, didn't anticipate what was going to happen to him? The answer is simple. He did.

1

Ten can be tricky. You're sandwiched like a slice of baloney between the humble single digits of childhood and the venerable knighthood of teendom, enlisted in a mandatory, three-year, high-stakes game of monkey in the middle; you're neither here nor there, unless you intercept the ball or turn thirteen. Some call this your "tweens"---too old for toys, too young for boys---but when, exactly, is anyone too old for toys?

Like a clogged toilet that won't stop running, my brain overflows with curiosity and primordial instinct, but I'm trapped like a prisoner in a child's body, gullible and dwarfish, and so eternally punished by the tyranny of moonstruck adults running amok. At the same time, it's hard to deny the benefits, the newfound respect, that nine simply could never confer. Double digits speak for themselves, and will always impress. Even the most highfalutin second grader can only cower with reverence at the unbridled maturity of a ten-year-old. It's true.

But ten, at the end of the day, is still only ten, an irrefutable improvement over nine, a step in the right direction, yes, but a far cry from the sophistication and polished glamour and infinite riches that come with being a teen. Thirteen is the real deal, the tippity-top, the pinnacle before the cynical, welcome to the big leagues, Mr. Number One Draft Pick.

There's one thing I'd better tell you right away, before we get ahead of ourselves; I collect lucky pennies. I'm obsessed with finding them and making wishes. For the granting of the privilege of making a wish, however, Abraham Lincoln's head must be facing up, no ifs, ands, or buts about it. I have so many lucky pennies at this point that I've stopped counting, but as any kindergarten kid can tell you, it's not about quantity, it's about quality, and in this particular case, the quality of the wish placed upon the penny. Mine are first-rate, top-of-the-line, grade A, ten-thousand-thread-count Egyptian cotton wishes.

Wishing is judged in three distinct categories: originality, degree of difficulty, and overall relevance to the world at large. And in that regard, you'd be hard pressed to find a finer, more experienced, more hardworking yet naturally gifted wish maker than me. I am a wish artist at heart, and a connoisseur in my head, and an aficionado through and through. I am the self-appointed world champion wish maker.

If you're cynical or skeptical, disagreeable or diabolical, if you're frightened of the unknown, like many people are, or if you're just a run-of-the-mill, crankety, crotchety (lacking in exercise), ill-humored, maladjusted, grown-up adult, then you may think it's childish to collect lucky pennies, even pointless. I can understand where you're coming from; sure, I'm hip to your simpleton, spoon-fed, Sesame Street understanding of the universe. No doubt you're just another innocent bystander caught in the crossfire of parental inadequacy, left for dead at the scene of a philosophical crime. So yes, from your perspective, I understand that lucky pennies aren't exactly tangible, they aren't traded on the New York Stock Exchange or even made out of copper anymore, but in my world pennies represent little windows into the universe of infinite possibilities, glimmers of hope that there's rhyme and reason behind all this nonsense.

It wouldn't surprise me at all to hear that some of the most notable and distinguished people the world's ever known have collected lucky pennies, or did when they were alive and could bend over. I'm sure Abraham Lincoln did, I know if I saw my face lying on the ground, minted in copper, I would pick it up. Bill Clinton definitely did, I'm not sure about Bush, I bet Obama does, although the Secret Service guys are probably always beating him to the punch, those bastards.

Luck is allusive, luck is beguiling, luck is enigmatic, luck is a lady, and you need to do whatever you can to get as much as you can as fast as you can, and just when you think you've got her she's gone. Like a dream that disappears when your alarm goes off, or a sumo wrestler covered in Jell-O, luck is impossible to wrap your arms around.

Here's a funny little tidbit about pennies; it costs two cents to make one. That's right. To manufacture one American penny, it actually costs two. The government claims it's because of the increased cost of materials and overhead and stuff, so to offset those costs somewhat, pennies are now only two percent copper and ninety-eight percent zinc. Taxpayers like you and me (one day) have to foot the bill for the sixty million bucks it's costing, this year alone, just to keep pennies in circulation. Which raises the question, do the wishing wells and piggybanks and penny arcades across the country really need the pennies? I'd rather the government just give the sixty million to me and get rid of pennies altogether, and this is coming from someone who loves pennies. Either that, or bite the bullet and outsource manufacturing to China for half the price. So what if it says Made in China on the back of the American penny? At least we wouldn't be losing our shirts on the deal.

In unrelated news, my Mom is a Buddhist (recently converted from Catholicism), and Buddhists don't believe in luck, which is hard for me to believe. I pretty much don't believe in anything but luck. I'm exaggerating, I believe in a lot of things, almost everything, actually, except for a few things here and there, like religion, for example, and eating animal livers, I will not do it.

Buddhists believe everything that happens in your life is the result of a physical or a spiritual cause. I think that means something like crime and punishment, or yin and yang, or slurp and burp. Simply put, there's a very good reason why everything happens, and when it happens to a Buddhist it's called karma, and karma is the result of cause and effect, in some form or another, from this or even a previous life, which is where things get particularly complicated.

If karma is what explains why good and bad things happen to Buddhists, then luck must explain what happens to everyone else. Why are some people always lucky and others almost never? The dictionary definition of luck is "good or bad fortune that occurs beyond one's control, for no explainable reason." Explainable being the key word there. I've been trying for years to acquire and control luck, or at least gently coax it my way. I want to harness luck like a cowboy and ride it like a bull through the streets of Pamplona. That's all I'm trying to accomplish here, a little control over my destiny, a friendly kick in Fortuna's tush, one penny at a time.

Luckily, I seem to possess a supernatural ability to spot a lucky penny, and in the least likely of places. It's uncanny, really, like finding a needle in a haystack (which I've done). From twenty-five yards away, I'm capable of spotting a lucky penny out of the corner of my eye with a sharpshooter's precision. It's pretty cool. I think my friends are impressed, or maybe not. I can be casually strolling along, having a conversation about the meaning of life or the merits of meatloaf while chewing gum and blowing bubbles, when out of nowhere there it is, across the street, near the gutter, under a dumpster, in the mouth of a dead rat, a brand-new penny, sparkling like the North Star, just for me to see. In fact, I'm what you might call a professional, because by definition I get paid to do it, and even though it's only pennies, it still counts, thus elevating me from amateur to professional status, which unfortunately disqualifies me from competing in the Olympics, or maybe not; I think it used to, but then they changed the rule so NBA players could all win gold medals and reclaim American basketball supremacy after a devastating loss to the Russkies at the '88 Games. None of that matters, though, not yet, because collecting lucky pennies isn't an Olympic sport, although ping-pong is, and curling and race walking are, so I'm hopeful.

You might be wondering what determines whether a penny is lucky or not. It's simple: it's lucky if you decide it's lucky. There's only one rule to follow: it must be found with Abraham Lincoln's head facing up. That's pretty much it. And it can be found, not just on the ground, but on the seat of a chair or the bottom of a school bus stair or in somebody's hair (it's happened). Just as long as its head is up, its chin is out, and it's a coin, you're in business.

Typically after spotting a lucky penny you bend down and pick it up, note the year it was minted, and make a wish. When you get home, you put it in your lucky penny jar (or repository in my case), sit back, and enjoy. My lucky penny repository is a gigantic glass barrel taller than me, capable of holding a million pennies or more. It is not to be confused with my regular-sized piggy bank, which is much smaller and pink and shaped like a pig with its head busted off, because I needed the money.

Despite having collected so many lucky pennies, I must confess that for some reason, though this doesn't make any sense, none of my wishes have come true, except for a few little ones that would have come true anyway, probably. It's okay. I'm not worried about this per se, not really, I firmly believe they'll all come true in due time, at least some of them. It just takes a while for wishes to materialize, right? It's not like ordering a pizza on the telephone and thirty minutes later you're burning the roof of your mouth with a slice of piping-hot pepperoni, not that I would know what that's like, since there's no pizza place that delivers anywhere close to the middle of nowhere, which is where I live.

I suspect making wishes is a lot like planting vegetables in a garden. They have to take root first before they can sprout, no doubt an elaborate process, and who am I to rush it, or even try to understand it? There's also the possibility that my entire lucky penny theory is total nonsense and my mom and Buddha are right. God, I certainly hope not. That would be extremely disappointing, to say the least.

I guess you could say I'm in religious limbo, spiritually speaking. I'm not a reformed Catholic turned Buddhist like my mom is, or Jewish like my dad was, or Muslim like my dentist, or Christian like my vice-principal, or a Mormon like my one friend, or a Scientologist like my other. If I had to make a decision today, right this second, I'd choose to be agnostic like Mark Twain and Albert Einstein---even Rob Van Dam is on the fence. In a multiple choice test, agnosticism would be like choosing none of the above, while atheism is more like crumpling up the test and throwing it in the garbage. It's true I've been accused of being a contrarian before. My mom thinks I'm always disagreeing with her, and with everyone, and for no particular reason, and I am sometimes, but in this particular case, and at this particular juncture in time and space, I'm not just rejecting religion for the sporting fun of it, I genuinely don't think it's good for your health. From my five-foot-two-and-a-half-inch perspective, religion is as ridiculous as a hippopotamus wearing polka-dot pajamas and pretending it's not. It's preposterous and hippocritical. What I believe in is luck, and lots of it.

2

My dad was pierced through the heart by a bolt of lightning in a freak thunderstorm six years ago. I consider this extremely bad luck. He was on the roof of our house adjusting the satellite dish when it happened. I think it's a heroic way to die, as far as dying goes. It's also tragically absurd, which I prefer to tragically grotesque or tragically mundane, but at the end of the day it's still tragic and he's still dead and we still have crappy TV reception. We live in a new house, though, in a new town, in a new state, with a new basic cable provider, so it's not his fault.

I've developed a radical new theory that explains how I will probably rebound from this unlucky occurrence to one day become the luckiest or second-luckiest person in the entire world, having arguably been the second-unluckiest so far (my dad having been the first). The science behind my new theory is strongly influenced by Isaac Newton's well-regarded third law of motion, which states that for every action there is an equal (or sometimes greater, in my personal and somewhat controversial version) reaction in the opposite direction. Meaning bad luck bounces back as good luck, the inevitable swinging of the pendulum, as I'm sure Isaac meant to say.

My father was a charming, imaginative, and passionate man, according to my mother, the quintessential entrepreneur with more energy than he knew what to do with, a wheelin' and dealin' American capitalist cowboy. "A lost relic of immigrant dreamers who have been replaced by a litigious society of unemployed lawyers and insurance salesmen," according to my unemployed uncle Tunafish, who has a law degree and no medical insurance, and lives in our barn.

As the story goes, my dad loved to play Frisbee, probably because his dad loved to play Frisbee. They were both master Frisbee throwers, remarkably ambidextrous and graceful. His freshman year of college my dad was unanimously elected president of the intramural Ultimate Frisbee team, and by senior year he was president of the National Collegiate Ultimate Frisbee Association.

When he graduated he decided, with his dad's encouragement and financial support, to start a Frisbee and boomerang company out of the garage, after miraculously convincing the U.S. and then the Australian and New Zealand governments' departments of education that the Frisbee and the boomerang, respectively, were the key to unlocking a child's untapped creativity and general well-being, both physical and mental. Financially this was a major coup for my old man, although his bold claims were never fully substantiated. He sold over thirteen million Frisbees, some kind of a record, along with quite a few boomerangs, and then, while eating an everything bagel with cream cheese and chives on the balcony of the Four Seasons in Marrakesh, he invented the Frisbee with the hole in the middle (before the Aerobie or the Skyro), which flew faster and farther, with more control, than any other flying disc in history, my mom says. But as the story also goes, my dad managed to lose his Frisbee fortune, including his patent and every last penny, in one particularly unlucky night at the high-stakes poker table in Lake Tahoe, Nevada.

A long time ago, before she was my mother, my mother was a poker dealer at Caesar's Palace. She was the best card dealer they ever had, she says, and because of that she was always stationed at the highest-stakes table. She was dealing the night my dad gambled away what could have been my Ultimate Frisbee fortune.

"I fell head over heels in love with him that night," she's told me a thousand times, "his unbreakable confidence, his eccentric style, the way he kept his cool as he lost all of his money. Literally all of it. He was charming and handsome and told funny jokes, despite the catastrophic bad luck hanging over him like a dark cloud. Losing hand after hand, over and over, he managed to keep his cool. I've never seen anything like it. The absolute worst luck of all time, if he had three jacks, he'd lose to three queens, and I was the one dealing the cards. He couldn't win and he couldn't stop, not a good position to be in, and for hours and hours it went on, and he never once won, not even one single hand. Eventually, he was betting millions on every flop of the card. And losing. He reminded me of *The Old Man and the Sea*, helplessly watching while the sharks pecked away at his marlin. Such poise and dignity and humility under duress are so rare in a man, especially a mustachioed man---he was somewhat famous for his handlebar mustache in those days. But more than anything, he was a gentleman through and through. He even tipped me his last hundred-dollar chip. After my shift ended he asked to walk me home, and on the way he politely covered a large puddle with his suede jacket. Courtesy, generosity, and valor like that just don't exist anymore." Then she'd choke up, every time, and the story ended.

My dad told me when I was three and a half that he was so taken by my mom's dazzling green eyes and luminous skin and overall good vibe that he hadn't entirely realized what he was doing. He was so fixated on my mom that he fell into a trance, a fantasy so intense he couldn't control what was happening around him, "just like a bad dream that refuses to obey your simplest request," is what he said if I remember correctly---I was young.

In his defense, my mom admits she might have accidentally hypnotized him with her mesmerizing dexterity. According to Uncle Tunafiash, she was one of the best card shufflers of all time. She could shuffle a deck a dozen different ways. She was faster and infinitely more elegant than the Shuffle Master 3000 machines that finally replaced her. She specialized in the riffle shuffle, but she could do the weave, pile, and Hindu like nobody's business.

I've spent gazillions of hours analyzing all this, and I've concluded that if it cost my dad his entire Frisbee fortune for the chance to charm my mom into marrying him, which eventually resulted in me, then it was worth it.

3

Bumpkinville, Montana, is exactly right in the middle of nowhere, with a population of 1234, and that includes the cows and the chickens. Despite its geographic isolation, its lack of modern sophistication, and its cultural nondiversity, it remains a quaint country western mountain town, a lovely place to spend one's formative years. Architecturally, it is an enchanting mixture of classic Greek, Native American, and Scandinavian influences.

The town underwent a freak economic turnaround following a paleontology conference held here in the 1980s. What began innocently enough ended in a late-night impromptu dig/dance party, during which some of the most important dinosaur bones ever discovered were excavated, including a ten-foot penile bone from a gargantuan Tyrannosaurus Rex. Oddly, this detail was omitted from the otherwise brilliantly directed and superbly acted AFI Top One Hundred classic *Jurassic Park*. Had TRex been anatomically correct in its portrayal, I think the movie would have been even better, especially in a new 3-D release, can you imagine!

I don't exactly live in Bumpkinville; technically, I live on the outskirts in a house next to a river by a hill adjacent to an endless forest in the boondocks of Bumpkinville, approximately a million miles away from anyone else. Sometimes it's nice being completely isolated from other human beings (not counting my mom or Tunafish), and other times it's painfully boring and unbearably lonely.

My mom relocated us five years ago as a way of starting over. "A new beginning," she said. "We get to write a new story for ourselves, maybe a comedy this time instead of a tragedy, plus Bumpkinville is safe and affordable with lots of clean air to breathe. What's not to like?"

My house is divided into two parts. Half is a more traditional Lincoln Log wooden cabin, and the other half is built entirely out of rocks from the river. My uncle claims to have built it himself, one rock at a time. He lives in the barn now, and his name wasn't always Tunafish, that's just what he decided to legally change it to, but if I call him Jeremiah, he'll murder me in cold blood, "Truman Capote style," he says. So I call him Tunafish. It's easier.

To get to school on time, I have to ride forty-five minutes on the school bus, and it takes fifteen minutes or so to walk from my bedroom to the bus stop, which makes it about an hour commute each way every day. Enough time to read a book or two a week, on average, depending on how many pages it is, or pictures there are.

If I didn't live so far away, I could sleep an extra hour every morning, and multiplied over the course of my life, including bus rides home, that would add up to a staggering amount of sleep I'm losing, probably an entire year or two of my life spent in a big yellow bus on the road to nowhere.

Do you know what a mayfly is? It's a little bug whose entire life is only one day long, sometimes less. Yet mayflies miraculously manage to get married and have kids and extramarital affairs, and in some cases even get divorced, all in about thirty minutes or less, presumably making the most out of what could have otherwise been a dismally brief existence.

On the other end of the life-span spectrum we have the grand master champion of the world for living the longest. It's a special jellyfish that is considered, in some neighborhoods, biologically immortal, just like a vampire. It surprises me that there isn't already a blockbuster film about these creatures. Imagine the *The Little Mermaid* meets *Twilight,* starring charismatic jellyfish with silky hair and sullen expressions, in 3-D.

I skipped kindergarten because I was in a rush, so graduating from elementary school was perhaps more meaningful for me than it was for the other kids. It signified that I had officially secured my place amongst a herd of wild animals born a year before me and understandably skeptical of life's anomalies, including myself. I could have probably skipped a few more grades while I was at it, but I feared the social complications.

Entering middle school was the inspiration for a major entrepreneurial revelation. I suddenly had an insatiable determination to be rich and powerful, and as quickly as possible.

I was given my very own sliver of prime real estate in the form of a small red aluminum locker with a combination lock and a water-fountain view. Within minutes of memorizing my combination I was hit with a brilliant idea. Instead of wasting my locker space on unnecessary personal junk like my books and jacket and lunch box and stinky socks, I could fill it with candy and toys and irresistible knickknacks, like finger skateboards and Garbage Pail Kids.

I added a two-hundred-and-fifty-percent markup and turned my locker into an ultra profitable 7-Eleven with almost none of the overhead. My profit margin and EBITA (earnings before interest, taxes, and amortization) were through the roof and growing each month. I was flush with cash, *Malcolm in the Middle* money, as my friend Mosquito liked to joke.

At lunchtime I was a hero. I could have anything I wanted in the cafeteria: extra milk not a problem, make it chocolate, slice of pizza, chili fries, some Jell-O, a cookie, a brownie, it was only money. My pockets were overflowing with cash and it felt good, I was like a rapper without the profanity. I was living the American Dream. I even bought a new Schwinn with a basket and a bell.

After a few weeks I started to wonder why I couldn't expand my locker-store empire into a national or even international retail chain. I was thinking of calling it Willy Nilly's, after myself, but just as I was about to branch out and into a friend's locker on the far side of the school, I was busted in an undercover sting operation led by Vice-principal Schmutz, also an amateur taxidermist and all-around propeller-headed ding-a-ling dipstick and doofus. He accused me of improper and possibly even illegal use of school property, along with misdemeanor tax evasion charges, same thing that happened to Al Capone. I was sentenced to one month of detention; Capone got eleven years in Alcatraz.

The tax evasion charges were later dropped, in large part because my mom passed out in Mr. Schmutz's office. She had been pleading and pleading for leniency without any luck, and then, in a simple twist of fate, she fainted like a Mexican soap opera star, bumping her head on the antlers of Schmutz's enormous stuffed moose, which wasn't hanging on the wall where any reasonable person would put a piece of taxidermy; no, it was planted smack-dab in the middle of the office, and it wasn't just a furry head and some antlers, it was the entire moose standing on all fours with a big creepy smile on its face, a safety hazard if ever there was one.

My mom was okay, luckily, except for a scratch on her cheek. Mr. Schmutz was required to remove his life-size taxidermies from his office, which included, in addition to the moose, a skunk and a squirrel and a saber-toothed tiger. The rest of the charges were dropped, but I still had to serve my one month of detention, and my budding locker-store business was permanently shut down.

I considered contesting the ban to the regional school board or taking it all the way to the Supreme Court if necessary, but my mom wouldn't let me. I had to sell my bike and go back to brown-bagging it with a thermos by day, tap water and homework by candlelight at night, to save electricity. After a few months without a steady income my piggy bank went belly up. I had to completely bust it open just to help my mom pay for groceries, specifically tropical-flavored Capri Suns, crunchy Skippy peanut butter, and frosted cherry Pop-Tarts.

My mom and I had been in various states of financial ruin since my dad died. I was more broke than her since she had a job, just not a good one, but she had to support me, herself, and her brother, Uncle Tunafish. At least I had the sixth grade to fall back on, but that wouldn't last forever. I wanted more, I craved adventure, I wanted to change the world, to make it better and more fun, like in a high-scoring game of Roller Coaster Sim City, but I needed money. I was restless to grow up and get a job and a dog and a credit card and a mortgage and a mustache and be taken seriously for once, but first I needed an innovative idea, a new plan of some kind, a scheme, an inspiration, a rainbow, a four-leaf clover, a fortune cookie, a wishbone, a friendly smile, a passing wave, a subtle glance, something, anything. Please.

And then, right on cue, as if Chris Elwood from the fourth season of *Punk'd* was pranking me, a sparkling penny screamed from across the playground, "Come and get me, Willy!" So I shuffled over and picked it up. Abraham Lincoln never looked so good, and this one was born the same year as me, which, I forgot to mention, makes for twice as lucky a penny.

I took a moment to carefully consider my wish, and then I closed my eyes and squeezed the penny tight and made that wish with all my might. And if you absolutely must know, I mean if you're going to beseech me to death, I'll just tell you. I wished that I was the richest, funniest, and most powerful person in the world, in charge of everything, right away, which may sound like two or three wishes, but it's not, it's just one big wish, trust me, I'm a professional.

4

A sixth-grade advanced English class that feels more like a Jungian psychology class, with bits and pieces of game theory and string theory and conspiracy theory thrown in for good measure, isn't typically found in a middle school curriculum these days. In this respect, Bumpkinville was astoundingly progressive. And it was all because of one particularly eccentric and wonderfully debonair forty-five-year-old super genius, distinguished sci-fi writer, Town Council member, and English teacher extraordinaire, Mr. Bob Dobalina. He liked to stand with his back to the class scribbling incomprehensible words onto the chalkboard. His students, time and again, were rapt with anticipation---at least I was, despite his track record for overshooting the audience.

It's fair to say that Mr. Dobalina was my all-time favorite teacher ever, hands down and by a mile. He wore bow ties and could play the accordion and had written a number of very long books about civilizations in faraway galaxies, and he could juggle better than a Ringling Bros. and Barnum & Bailey clown. He was the best teacher in the world, no question about it. Not to mention that he's a certifiable genius, with a framed Mensa certificate on his desk to prove it. Sometimes he lets me dust it.

Mr. Dobalina knows pretty much everything there is to know and would pretty much make the best mayor Bumpkinville could ever hope for. I keep telling him to run. He always flips it around on me and says that I should run. Ha. Like that's realistic? He's being facetious, I'm sure, because obviously no one's gonna vote for me; I have no money to lobby for power or buy TV commercials, and I've never even been to a political party.

Mr. Dobalina could have taught at a fancy university or joined the CIA or worked at CAA, but he chose to live in a small town and teach middle school kids instead. He says he has a bigger impact on the world that way. What a guy. Off the record, just between us, I'd rather do Mr. Dobalina's homework assignments than hang out with my friends, although I would never admit that to them unless I specifically wanted them to hate me.

Today Mr. Dobalina broke his riveting silence with a lecture about two words, conundrum and paradox. "These are two powerful words used to explain and discuss some of the most complex and profound questions in the universe. They're also simple words used in poems and to explain unsolvable puzzles. These words are commonly misunderstood or confused with one another. Does anyone happen to know the meaning of these words? Either? No one?" Taking off his thick orange-rimmed glasses, he rubbed his eyeballs and squinted at his students for signs of life. "Anyone care to hazard a guess?"

The class was as silent as a mime in a mortuary, not a peep. As usual, nobody raised a hand, so it was up to me as sacrificial lamb. Even though I was a little fuzzy on the actual meaning of the words---to be honest, I didn't have a clue---I couldn't let Mr. Dobalina down. He pointed to me. "Willy, which word do you know?"

Then it came to me. "If I'm not mistaken the conundrum is a North African tribal drum used for religious ceremonies and beheadings?"

"You are drastically mistaken." Mr. Dobalina marveled to himself, then slid his orange glasses back up the bridge of his nose. "Perhaps you're confusing conundrum with the candombe drum, Willy, which is from Uruguay, and completely different. But good try."

"Thanks," I said.

"A conundrum," he continued, "is a confusing problem or a riddle, sometimes even with a pun for an answer. Conundrums aren't always meant to be answered, sometimes they're just meant to be posed and pondered. Here's an example: if money grows on trees, why do banks have branches?"

Blank stares from everyone.

"All right, here's a conundrum that uses a pun. What's the difference between a cat and a comma?" Beat, beat, beat. "A cat has claws at the end of its paws, and a comma is a pause at the end of a clause."

Everyone sighed a sigh of polite confusion and naive optimism at the distant possibility of it all making sense one day.

Mr. Dobalina sighed too. "All right, how about a paradox? Would anyone like to take a stab at that?"

Naturally I raised my hand.

"Anyone other than Willy?" Mr. Dobalina said.

The class had no imagination; it was embarrassing.

Mr. Dobalina pointed to me.

"I think I might really know this one," I said. "Isn't a paradox a large bird that lives in an underwater cave along the eastern coast of Australia?" For an extra touch of realism, I scratched my chin and added, "Just south of Perth?"

"Actually, Willy, miraculously, that is almost an example of a paradox. It's not, but you were so close it pains me. Let me explain. Birds, as we all know, live on the land and fly in the air and consequently don't live underwater and swim. So to suggest that a bird swims and lives on the east coast of Australia but also south of Perth, which is on the west coast, is a multiple self-contradicting statement, impressively, yet it's not quite a paradox, because it's total nonsense and simply not true. A paradox is a statement or a proposition that seems self-contradictory or absurd but in reality expresses a possible truth. 'When pigs fly' would be a paradox if it were true, but it's not, so it's not."

For some reason the abstract contradictory concept of a paradox was exciting to me. I felt like it was about to become my new favorite word. A bubbling euphoric feeling rose up in my stomach and into my chest. I was dizzy with optimism. It was a fun word to say and to hear and to think about. It had it all. I wouldn't be surprised if it was the most envied word in the entire dictionary.

Mr. Dobalina kept talking. "Another example of a paradox is, what happens when an unstoppable force meets an unmovable object? That's the classic superhero paradox. Or, the more I learn the less I know, Socrates' famous knowledge paradox. Or try this one on for size. It's by a famous philosopher with a big mustache named Friedrich Nietzsche, and he asked the really big questions, like 'Is man merely a mistake of God's? Or is God merely a mistake of man's?'"

Mr. Dobalina was unfazed by our complete incomprehension. He forged on with his lecture. "Gandhi once, with infinite wisdom, wrote that 'whatever you do will be insignificant, but it's very important that you do it.' Does that make any sense to anyone?"

Everyone shook their heads, mostly to the left and right, with a few insincere ups and downs. Searching for additional clarity and attention, I asked, "Is homework a paradox?"

"No."

"Why not?"

"Because homework is an oxymoron, actually, not a paradox. Thank you for pointing that out, Willy. An oxymoron, everyone, is a figure of speech that contradicts itself, like 'pretty ugly,' or 'minor crisis,' or my favorite, 'the Civil War.'"

The entire class had been hypnotized into the Twilight Zone, never to return, but not me; I had a chainsaw, protective goggles, and a Segway, and I was determined to get out of this intellectual forest of words unscathed. No matter what, I would survive, regardless of the possible brain damage that might come from this relentless bombardment of sophisticated information.

Mr. Dobalina scribbled two new sentences onto the chalkboard. "The next sentence I write is true. The previous sentence I wrote is false."

The class scratched their chins in unison. Smoke billowed from their ears. But I was impervious. I was a force field of focus and concentration.

"Let's try this one on," Mr. Dobalina said. "It's easy. Everyone knows who Pinocchio is, right?"

Everyone nodded their heads, beaming with pride, so happy to finally know something.

"And we all know that if Pinocchio tells a lie then his nose will grow, right? So what happens if Pinocchio says, 'My nose will be growing'?"

I raised my hand. Everyone should know this, I thought.

Mr. Dobalina waved me off with a casual smile and answered his own question. "Since Pinocchio isn't lying when he says that his nose will be growing, then his nose won't grow, that's the catch, but if his nose doesn't grow then he is lying, so then it will grow, but if it grows then it wasn't a lie because he said it would be growing and it did, and on and on and on. This is called the Pinocchio paradox."

It wasn't pretty, the class was on the verge of death by confusion, a torturous way to go.

"Which one came first, class, the chicken or the egg?"

"The chicken," I blurted out, having recently skimmed through an old *National Geographic* article about chickens. "The Red Junglefowl, Mr. Dobalina, if I'm not mistaken, is generally believed to be the predecessor of the modern chicken, as we know it. So there you go, it was a chicken after all. Problem solved."

"I'm impressed, Willy, *National Geographic* magazine is so out of fashion these days, good for you. However, recent DNA testing suggests that the modern chicken is actually a hybrid bird, descendant of both the Red Junglefowl and the Grey Junglefowl. By virtue of its being a hybrid, the implication is that the egg existed before the chicken in this particular case."

Duly noted, I thought. "So what about people, Mr. Dobalina?" I said, raising the temperature in the room. "Who came first, the mother or the baby, and is a man even required after we reach a certain level of DNA understanding with manipulation capabilities, and does that mean men might one day become superfluous to the evolutionary process? And if they do, then is it possible that men have resisted women's equality, historically speaking, on an unconscious level because of our inevitable fear of obliteration by them?"

It's wasn't like I had actually considered this new theory of mine before now, this was hot off my presses, but wow, I think I might have stumbled onto something.

"That's a charming new theory, Willy. Let's pick it up next week, shall we? Okay, class, your homework assignment for the weekend is very easy, yet terribly hard. It's also far too important to be taken seriously. Here it is: I want you to find something bad and make it good. Got it? Any questions? Okay. Good. Go. Take something bad and make it good. Class dismissed."

And the bell rang at that exact moment. It was so impeccably timed with his hand gestures and vocal emphasis that I immediately felt as if he had spent months, maybe even years, rehearsing this speech with an acclaimed choreographer. But where would you find an acclaimed choreographer in Bumpkinville? Impossible, but still, this was laser-cut, Egyptian-pyramid precision timing. Where did Mr. Dobalina find the time to rehearse and still teach all his other classes and write science fiction books and practice juggling staplers and attend Town Council meetings and do everything else that he no doubt did on the side? Another unsolvable conundrum, I guess, or a paradox, or perhaps it was just a coincidence, or what Carl Jung described as synchronicity (a meaningful coincidence). There is one thing I know for sure. Mr. Dobalina was in a meditative groove today, like he was riding a barrel in Waikiki, totally in tune with his toes and the class and the board and the wave overhead and the school bell about to ring. He was hangin' ten on the chalkboard with his mind, all-knowing and wise, surfing through time and space.

5

On the middle school playground, by the tetherball courts, across from the monkey bars, catty-corner to the seesaws, I stood in a triangle formation with my two best friends, Tilo and Mosquito, kicking a Hacky Sack back and forth. Mosquito was pretty good, me not so good, and Tilo was so-so. My arms worked better than my legs. I had inherited my parents' dexterity, but not their agility, unless they were also agility-challenged, in which case I did, but I digress; I was more of a tetherball man myself.

The sky was purple, orange, and gray, and getting darker by the second. I could smell a storm brewing. If we were in Kansas we would have run for the cellar of the closest farmhouse, but here in Bumpkinville the most we feared was a freak spring hailstorm, which was not only survivable but Hacky Sackable. Rain or shine, we would stick it out till the recess bell rang.

It just so happened that on this particular day our conversation was more mind-numbingly mundane than normal, right up until an epiphany fell out of the sky and nearly squashed me.

Tilo: You know that cryogenic thingamajig is this weekend.

Willy: This weekend?

Tilo holds a flyer up for the event. It reads: Saturday, high noon, Town Square, Live on CNN.

Willy: We should go.

Mosquito: Really? Sounds kind of boring.

Willy: Immortality bores you?

Mosquito: No such thing. Everyone dies.

Willy: Well, I can't speak for all of humanity, but I intend to attain immortality, and then build a tricked-out flying saucer with a bright green shag carpet and a Jacuzzi and a Florider---it's like a treadmill for surfing--- and a frozen yogurt machine with a topping bar, and then I can spend an eternity exploring every last nook and cranny of the unknown universe. Oh, and you probably won't be invited, FYI.

Mosquito: Good.

Willy: Great.

Mosquito: Awesome.

Willy: Tilo, you can come.

Tilo: How can you live forever if you're frozen the whole time?

Mosquito: Yeah, sounds more like a pricy Popsicle to me.

Willy: I guess the major difference is that if you freeze yourself before you actually die, you can preserve your body and presumably your brain until doctors have discovered cures to all diseases and have actually reversed the aging process so you can live forever. It's like pausing a movie versus stopping it and having to start all the way back at the beginning.

Tilo: Sounds cool.

Willy: Guess how much it costs.

Tilo: A hundred grand?

Willy: Try ten million.

Tilo: WHAT!!! For ten million, I will stick whoever it is in my spare freezer downstairs in the cellar. Seriously, I could clear out the ice cream and last year's elk meat within the hour. With ten million buckeroos, baby, I could buy a cotton-candy machine and a hot-air balloon and float to Bora Bora, to begin with.

Willy: Ten million doesn't get you what it used to, not anymore.

Tilo: I could really use the money. You think there's any way we could convince the guy to get frozen in my basement fridge?

Willy: No.

Tilo: Mosquito, what do you think?

Mosquito: You mean give you ten million bucks to go in your freezer next to your elk meat and ice cream? I really doubt it.

Willy: Why do you need money so bad?

Mosquito: Do you have a gambling problem?

Tilo: I can't say. I mean I'm not supposed to. I really shouldn't. I promised I wouldn't. Please don't make me. If I tell you you have to promise me that you won't tell anyone. Nobody. I can't believe I'm telling you guys this, but my mom accidentally bought a huge bag of oranges yesterday that turned out to be a huge bag of lemons!

Mosquito: Is this some kind of stupid joke, Tilo?

Tilo: My mom made me promise not to tell anyone.

Mosquito: So it isn't a joke?

Tilo: No, it's my reality! I'm gonna be drinking lemonade for the rest of my life. If my parents don't get divorced over this first.

Mosquito: Fruit merchants are sneaky sonofaguns, I've always known that. I bet they painted all the lemons orange just to trick her into buying them so they could get a higher price. That happened to my cousin once.

Bastards.

Willy: Come on, nobody paints a lemon orange, that's lunacy.

Tilo: I'm sad to say that they do.

Mosquito: Scary what this world is coming to.

Tilo: Not only were they individually painted orange, they were also in a bright orange nylon bag, so my mom just assumed they were oranges. Who can blame her?

Mosquito: I can blame her.

Willy: But you said the same thing happened to your cousin.

Mosquito: It did, and I blamed him too. Never assume!

Willy: He's right, it's true, you should never assume. You should also contact the Better Business Bureau right away. I think it might be illegal to sell orange lemons in orange bags. If nothing else, it's false advertising.

Mosquito: Sounds to me like a bait-and-switch operation.

Willy: A confidence job?

Tilo: Let's just say that my dad is pissed.

Willy: I think I just had an epiphany.

Mosquito: I don't smell anything.

Willy: An epiphany is a sudden intuitive realization, Mosquito, not a fart.

Mosquito: I was kidding, I know what an epiphany is.

Willy: We should open a lemonade stand to help Tilo get rid of his lemons. We can set up on Saturday morning and sell lemonade to all the tourists who'll be in town for the cryogenic freezing. The timing is perfect! And this is exactly what Mr. Dobalina was talking about. Taking something bad, or at least something that seems bad, like a big bag of orange lemons in this case, and making it good. When life hands you lemons, as they say...

No response from the peanut gallery.

Willy: You make lemonade! Hello, you guys never heard that expression before? It's famous.

Tilo: But I don't like lemonade.

Willy: Who cares if you like lemonade, Tilo, you should be jumping up and down for joy. This is the answer to all your problems. I've just hit three birds with one stone!

Tilo: What in the world does that mean?

Willy: It means I solved your parents' relationship problems, I did our homework for Mr. Dobalina, and I made us some potentially serious money, all by selling lemonade on Saturday. The only problem I can foresee at this point is counting all of our money, because we're gonna make so much of it I can almost taste it.

Mosquito: I only drink caramel frappuccinos and white chocolate pumpkin pie decaffeinated mochas with whipped cream and sprinkles. That's just me.

Tilo: I didn't know they made white chocolate pumpkin pie mochas.

Mosquito: Does Ringo play the kazoo?

Willy: Is that a rhetorical question? Because you guys sound like a couple of communists right now. Don't you know it's anti-American not to like lemonade? Treason, I believe. Especially if it's homemade with lots of sugar and it's sold by adorable kids like us. Who doesn't like sugar or kids? I'll tell you who, communists!

Tilo: It's true, communists don't like kids.

Mosquito: Personally, the only person I personally know who actually likes lemonade is my grandma, but she also likes gefilte fish sandwiches, which are dee-scust-ing. Have you ever tried a gefilte fish sandwich? I didn't think so.

Willy: Is your grandmother Jewish?

Mosquito: Does SpongeBob live in Bikini Bottom?

Willy: But I always thought you were a Scientologist. I mean, you have that huge poster of L. Ron Hubbard hanging in your kitchen, I just assumed.

Mosquito: I am a Scientologist. My parents switched religions two years ago, but not my grandma, she's stubborn, said she was too old to start over. But my dad says Scientology is way more relevant than anything else out there, and more practical than Jewishness. Apparently, Scientology is based on an awesome super-fast-paced sci-fi thriller and *New York Times* bestseller, versus the more solemnly written, dense and depressing Old Testament. My dad also likes to point out that *Battlefield Earth* isn't Mitt Romney's favorite novel for nothing.

Tilo: Who's Mitt Romney?

Willy: Wait, are you a Republican too?

Mosquito: Maybe. Does it matter?

Willy: Yeah, kind of.

Mosquito: Why?

Willy: I'm just messing with you. I'm bipartisan, obviously.

Mosquito: Well, it's too late anyway, because I've already signed a billion-year contract.

Willy: With the Republicans?

Mosquito: No. With the Church of Scientology, you idiot.

Willy: I know a guy who knows a lawyer who can probably get that reduced if you want. A billion's a lot.

Mosquito: Can we talk about something else?

Willy: Guys! The lemonade stand is our destiny, our fate, our future depends on it. It's in the stars. It can't be a coincidence, Tilo, that your mom bought a big bag of lemons on the same exact weekend that we need to sell lemonade at the cryogenic freezing. Can it?

Mosquito: That's exactly what it could be. That's what a coincidence is.

Willy: I think it's divine intervention, maybe synchronicity. Wait a second, quiet everyone, I think I can hear L. Ron Hubbard trying to tell me something right now.

Tilo: I don't hear anything.

Mosquito: Of course you don't hear anything, Tilo.

Willy: Yeah, because you're both talking and not listening, but I was listening and I heard what L. Ron Hubbard was saying.

Tilo: What did he say?

Willy: He said to sell lemonade on Saturday.

Mosquito: Ha.

Willy: And he said to at least watch *Battlefield Earth* on Blu-ray if we can't find the time to read the thousand-page book, which he actually admitted could use a serious rewrite.

Mosquito: I don't believe that.

Willy: I was surprised by that part too. But that's what he said.

Tilo: Seriously, Willy, I'd like to sell my mom's lemons more than anyone, but who's gonna buy our lemonade if there's a Starbucks right next door?

Willy: Let me put it to you like this, Tilo. If we don't do something drastic with your lemons, you're gonna be stuck eating them for a billion years. Is that what you want?

Tilo: I'm not a Scientologist, Willy, I'm Mormon, you know that.

Willy: Do you want to get rich beyond your wildest dreams so you never have to worry about money ever again? Do you want to save your family from eternal embarrassment and damnation? Or not?

Tilo drops his head in defeat.

Willy: Then it's settled, we'll sell lemonade on Saturday. We can split the money three ways, even though it's my idea, and then live the good life, high on the hog, happily ever after, even after we pay Tilo's mom back for the lemons, plus any other related expenses.

Mosquito: Do you even know how to make lemonade?

Willy: Yeah, of course I do. It can't be that hard, it's just sugar and water and ice and little drink umbrellas, right? Am I forgetting anything?

6

Turning lemons into lemonade is like turning pennies into dollars or pessimism into optimism or communism into capitalism or brine shrimp into Sea-Monkeys. All you need is determination, perseverance, and patience, and anything is possible. Success, at the end of the day, is only a relative concept, which means everybody fails and succeeds simultaneously at everything they do, it all just depends on your point of view, and from mine, a lemonade stand seemed like a great idea, a throwback to a golden era, a friendly nod to a lost generation, to a time when we all still believed in the American Dream and Santa Claus.

Lemonade stands are synonymous with happy times, symbolic of a nation filled with open-minded, picnic-eating, sun-block-wearing, firework-blasting, fun-loving people, with a McDonald's and a millionaire on every corner. Times have changed, as they do. People aren't as dewy-eyed anymore. It's too bad, really, but considering the never-ending barrage of bad news, I'm not surprised. Even in Bumpkinville, morale was low. Cynicism was on high alert. And the truth was, Mosquito and Tilo and I weren't a bunch of irresistible pigtailed little girls (figuratively speaking) anymore. The days of us skating by on our dimples and adorableness alone were gone.

We had furrows of worldliness, wrinkles of maturity, even a few whiskers (blond) here and there. We had an abundance of wisdom beyond our years, but we weren't cute anymore, not at all, not since about the time we hit double digits. In fact, if push came to shove, you might find some people who thought we were slightly off-putting, even unbecoming. Let's face it, we were this close to being certifiable Neanderthals, despite our peanut-sized frames and Velcro sneakers. Who in their right mind was gonna buy a glass of lemonade from us, hooligans and lepers who reeked of untrustworthiness, especially in this age of widespread corporate chicanery?

We might as well be selling plutonium Popsicles, because we were doomed to fail, kaput and kaplooey, we were chop suey. What if nobody was thirsty, or worse, what if everyone was thirsty but they chose to die of thirst rather than succumb to a glass of our organic, locally sourced, fair-trade lemonade? What was this world coming to? I was panicked.

Uncle Tunafish glanced at me in the passenger seat inquisitively, like he had just heard the thoughts inside my head, then turned back to the road

and continued driving while playing airplane out the window, his left arm
gliding and dangling in the wind, not a care in the world, catching flight
with his fingers as rudders, tilting and twirling and swooping around upside
down, nearly slipping into an irreversible nose dive but pulling out just in
time, no doubt the same way Orville and Wilbur must have when they were
learning to fly. Tunafish was no Wright brother, don't get me wrong, but he
was my mom's brother and he had a car and I usually needed a lift. A self-
described amateur botanist and professional unemployed lawyer, he wore
Birkenstocks, beads, and bell-bottoms most of the time. He had sparkling
green eyes, little ears, a big nose, and a wild "Jewfro," his word, not mine.
He was the unofficial poster child for modern-day hippies, or (as he
preferred to be referred to as) "an advocate of extreme liberalism." If you
had to put your finger on exactly why, it was probably his iPhone and
wireless earpiece, along with his not-for-profit web site and eternal
Kickstarter project devoted entirely to raising awareness of an unusual
psychotropic plant that only grows in one specific region on the planet,
where he also happens to own, with mixed feelings, two weeks' worth of an
undervalued, nontransferable, run-down, three-bedroom, two-bath, time-
share condominium with a surprisingly steep annual maintenance fee.

The radio was tuned to NPR, the only non-country station that ever
seemed to get reception. I wondered why country music had a monopoly
on the radio waves. Was it easier to transmit than other types? Maybe
because of its simplicity it took less bandwidth, which allowed it to be
received much farther away? Or maybe, because country music was so
popular, the radio stations that played it could afford more powerful
transmitting satellites, in which case I wouldn't be surprised if they were
also moonlighting for SETI (Search for Extraterrestrial Intelligence). That
made a lot of sense, aliens and country music, like two peas in a pod.
They're the perfect alibis for each other. Why didn't I notice this sooner? It
was so obvious. I'm so naive sometimes it scares me.

And then a cannon exploded in my mind. I felt like a Roman soldier
being ambushed by the Germanic war chief Arminius at the Battle of the
Teutoburg Forest. My own brain was waging war on me, shooting rapid-fire
hypothetical scenarios instead of bullets, like what if Snapple or Gatorade
or Coke or Capri Sun, with their infinite marketing budgets and fancy
offices and secret taste-testing focus groups and endangered-animal special
ingredients, decided to set up their own lemonade stand right next to mine?

What then? I'd be ruined.

And what if CNN did a last-minute undercover report on how I, personally, was a shining example of the moronic mediocrity and incompetence of tweens these days? I could hear the sound bite now as a reporter live on the scene smeared on her lipstick before flipping her hair like she was auditioning for a Head and Shoulders commercial, staring insincerely into the 20mm telephoto lens of a JVC video camera, and saying, "Willy Nilly and his posse of misfits standing beside him, from left to right Vito the Mosquito and Tilo the Burrito, have been apprehended, red-handed, caught in a web of delusion and deceit. Deceit on the general public for perpetrating one of the lamest and least original business ideas in recent history! Now back to you in the studio, Stormy Weathers."

The reporter was clearly off her rocker, on the lam from the loony bin. I mean, come on, really? I didn't know how to begin to respond to that, so I didn't, and since it was a purely hypothetical scenario in my head, nobody pressed me to.

An entrepreneur isn't worth a stick of Doublemint bubble gum if he doesn't follow his intuition, and since I hadn't been lobotomized yet by an Ivy League education and thirty years of reading the paper and watching the nightly news, I was lucky enough to still have my instincts intact and in tune. I didn't have to pay rent yet either, which was important and meant that I wasn't a puppet or under the influence of a special interest lobbyist--- just my mom. I didn't owe alimony, and I didn't have a credit card or any debt or years of regret to try and forget.

I had never almost failed so spectacularly in my life. My innocence and naïveté were in jeopardy with every squeeze of the lemon. What would Mr. Dobalina think? His star pupil, pal, and protégé botching the most important homework assignment of his life! I trembled at the thought. And the more and more I thought about it, the more and more cliché and downright trite this whole lemonade thing sounded. At best, it was a postmodern attempt at hipster credibility and easy money, at worst, a self-aware, lame, and obvious attempt to make a buck with a copycat, me-too concept and mediocre management. Mosquito and Tilo had tried to explain this to me beforehand, good friends that they are. They had said it loud and clear, "Lemonade isn't popular anymore," but I wouldn't listen. I was delirious. Blinded by ambition and a desperate need to succeed and be liked.

Let's face it, Starbucks was all anyone wanted these days, either that or a Red Bull, plain and simple. I must have lost my marbles on the playground that day. I can't remember ever being bamboozled by my brain like that before. Something had gone terribly wrong in my thought process. It seemed to me like a manufacturer's malfunction, what General Motors might call a lemon. The question remained: had my brain intentionally hornswoggled me, or was it an innocent malfunction? Was it even fair to blame my brain? I knew it wasn't my whole body's fault, which left my brain at fault by default. My fingers and my toes had nothing to do with it, clearly, so I can't blame them, although I'd love to. But is my brain me or am I my brain or am I not my brain or is it the same? Are we all just a bunch of brains walking around propped up on our shoulders? The answer, I guess, is probably yes.

It was about here, in my slightly neurotic and demoralizing philosophical rhyming and ranting, that I realized something. If time was money, then money was time, and if time was money, then it would probably have a rate of inflation or deflation like money did, so from my rough calculations, based on the rate of inflation over the last fifty years, I'm actually far older than the date on my birth certificate suggests. I'm light-years older, in fact, in the same way that a million dollars is worth far less now than it was fifty years ago, but in the case of time, inflation is inverted, so ten years old today is more like fifteen or sixteen used to be. If you acknowledge all of the technological, scientific, and communication developments that have taken place in the last century alone, you'll have to agree with me. For instance, the internet or CNN or the discovery of DNA or the invention of the NBA all make us, as a species, smarter, with a broader scope on the universe at large. In contrast, before these developments, life was less complicated. People weren't burdened with so much information, which equated to being younger in age, psychologically speaking. I wondered if I could prove this theory in a court of law, and if I could, would they let me drive home?

I pondered this question as Uncle Tunafish continued driving me to town in his run-down 1962 purple Volkswagen Beetle. Mosquito and Tilo were meeting me in Town Square so we could set up the now dreaded lemonade stand, which I had psyched myself out of in unprecedented fashion. I was nearly beside myself with self-doubt. I had "the willies," as my uncle liked to say. It was too late to cancel or I would have. I was stuck for so many reasons, mainly financial. I was in too deep. There was no turning back. I had real skin in the game, about twelve dollars. Rain, shine, or massive self-doubt, this show must go on. It was my fiduciary responsibility.

7

I had bought the lemons on credit from Tilo's mom and hired Wendy Wiggleman, an aspiring fourth-grade calligrapher, to make the signs. Wendy had earned a bit of a reputation for her work on Sally Weenerstein's student council campaign posters. Despite her mediocre math grades, Sally won the coveted position of class treasurer in a landslide entirely because of Wendy's superb poster work. The power of the media!

Wendy was an undeniable artiste of fancy lettering, which was why we decided to pay her top dollar. She drove a hard bargain too, and was incredibly persuasive. I was ready to walk at $4.75, but she was relentless, like a hungry baby tiger being kept from her mom and a salami sandwich for way too long, watch out.

The cryogenic freezing was scheduled to take place on a temporary stage constructed in the center of Town Square on a little plot of grass by a bench. A cheap banner, probably from Kinko's, hung above the stage: Cryonics Cryogenics, Safely Preserving Your Neighbors Since 2001. There were a few TV cameras and satellite news vans parked around the square.

I have always assumed I'd live forever, or at least a few thousand years, unless I was hit by a bus and run over. Most people throughout history have probably assumed the same thing, but in my particular case it just happened to be true as long as medical science continued to advance at the current rate, which it would under pretty much any scenario I could imagine. The only real problem I could forsee was the breaking of my precious heart when I least suspected it, but barring that, I should make it safely into triple digits and maybe all the way to the bonus rounds since I definitely wouldn't be dying from a disease or a broken-down old organ, what with organ transplants as common these days as root canals or rhinoplasties. Of course, that still left plenty of other ways to die, but there was only so much you could do. It would be comforting to see a cryogenic freezing firsthand, because in a worst-case scenario of epic medical calamity and worldwide economic depression, that was my backup plan, the backup to my backup being Tilo's freezer.

Although the actual freezing wasn't scheduled until noon, we arrived in town on Saturday at the crack of 9:45 a.m. This was a miracle, considering that Tunafish was borderline nocturnal, which made mornings before 3:00 p.m. difficult.

The grass was damp with dew from the night's frost, which was beginning to melt away as the sun peeked its smiling face up and over the Bumpkinville valley. I had a thousand caterpillars crawling around in my stomach, which is an unsettling feeling, especially when they begin their metamorphosis into full-blown butterflies, which feels like popcorn popping and buzzing around like bumper cars in your belly, or like a mosh pit from a Seattle music venue in the nineties.

It was an eerily familiar feeling, the same as from field day in fifth grade, but in this case the crown jewel of events wasn't the infamous egg toss or the classic tug-of-war over a mud puddle, but instead a mad territory dash like it was 1889 to claim a piece of prime real estate. I was determined to find the ultimate plot and set up shop before anyone else. I had done some research, and in most cases success for a retail operation came down to three very simple components: location, location, location. Ideally, I wanted to avoid being in the same sight line as Starbucks and still be close enough to the stage for good TV exposure.

I also needed some time to get all my ducks in a row. Baby ducklings usually swim in a straight line behind the mother duck, and if any of them stray too far she tells them to get back in line, and by extension that made me mother duck for the day, and Mosquito and Tilo my ugly little ducklings.

A lemonade stand is a fairly straightforward proposition. It requires seventeen ingredients: lemons, sugar, water, a pitcher (or two), a squeezer, ice cubes (ice balls are even better), disposable paper cups, a bowl to display the lemons in, a table to put them on, a tablecloth (a classic red-and-white-checkered pattern goes nice with the lemons), a sign that says Lemonade and a sign that says how much it costs to buy the lemonade (in my case, one dollar a glass, five glasses for three dollars, ten glasses for five dollars, or a pitcher for ten dollars), plus a money box to keep the money in (it's good to remember that Thomas Jefferson $2 bills get $3 of emotional value), and a coin bank for making change, with at least twenty dollars' worth. Last but not least, little drink umbrellas, a stroke of genius on my part. All you need to sell lemonade are those items and a smile, and a chair or three if you want to sit down.

Except, apparently, if you live in Bumpkinville and it's cryogenic freezing day. On this particular day, in this particular situation, you are also going to need a town permit, can you believe this, that takes thirty days from now to get, a permit allowing for the conditional sale of food and/or beverages from street carts or temporary food stands.

Talk about total bogusness, this was the proverbial shakedown. This was more than a monkey wrench in my plan, it was a downright thermonuclear meltdown, a code red alert, a catastrophe in the making, pretty much exactly my worst fear come true. We had just finished putting the final touches on what looked to me like the finest lemonade stand the world's ever known when a police officer in a one-piece jumpsuit and a Charlie Chaplin mustache casually caught wind of our humble enterprise. It was immediately obvious that this was not a good thing. You could almost see his cerebral cortex fluttering with confusion: who, what, where, why, and how did these three midget aliens in kid costumes manage to set up a lemonade stand right in the middle of Town Square and under his nose? I watched him stand with one hand on his hip and the other scratching his chin. Then he lifted his aviator sunglasses and squinted his eyes at me and licked his lips and marched over and barked like a Rottweiler, "What in the world do you little rascals think you're doing?!"

I took a deep breath, reminded myself there wasn't a lot of crime in these parts, and carefully explained what seemed perfectly obvious already, thanks to Wendy's impeccable calligraphy. After completely ignoring my simple explanation, the officer threatened to "shut you down, toss you in the clink, and throw away the key!"

"What's the clink?" I asked.

"The same thing as the can or the cooler or the big house," he said, poking me in the chest, "somewhere you don't want to be."

"Does this have anything to do with golf?" I asked.

"No, you little twerp, I'm talking about the illegal placement of a beverage dispensary booth on city property. You need a permit to occupy this space, and failure to obtain one is a misdemeanor offense cited in the penal code, number 8675309, punishable by up to one year in jail and/or a two-hundred-and-fifty-thousand-dollar fine. How would you like that?"

This seemed excessive for selling lemonade, or rather, for the hope of selling lemonade, since we hadn't sold a single glass yet. But having seen several seasons of *The Sopranos*, I didn't panic. I had a pretty good idea what was going on: he was looking for a handout, a bribe, some payola, as they called it in these parts. So I wasted no time attempting to buy the policeman's goodwill with a slyly placed two-dollar bill cupped neatly in the palm of my hand.

They sure make it look easy on TV, because no matter how hard I tried, I couldn't even come close to greasing the policeman. He just wouldn't shake my hand. Without even realizing it, he refused. Like his hand was magnetically opposed to mine somehow.

As a last-ditch effort, it seemed like a good idea to casually lean toward him as far as I could, like I was looking over a cliff but was scared to get too close to the edge, and then, just before I lost my balance, I lunged for his hand to pass him the cash, but he had catlike reflexes and jumped back, deftly avoiding any physical contact with me altogether.

He almost slapped the cuffs on me for that one. He characterized it as a thwarted lunge for his laser gun, which I adamantly denied, claiming to have lost my balance, which happens to everyone, I reminded him, even a funambulist.

There was nothing I could do to save our lemonade stand. I let him know in uncertain terms that he was being "overly persnickety about all of this beverage permit nonsense," and he let me know that "rules are rules, buster, and who are you to break them?"

He had me there. Then he held his forefinger and thumb about an inch apart and said I was that close to a ride on the back of his Segway if I kept it up. I thanked him again for his good work protecting Bumpkinville from dangerous criminals like myself, and also for the critical reasoning skills he had superbly displayed today, and he told me I could "shove it, buster," and I didn't blame him for that, but I did blame him for ruining my entire life. Having started the day by conquering and claiming what was arguably the most desirable retail location in Bumpkinville's history, I found it massively deflating to be forced to concede my land before selling a single glass of lemonade.

The kind policeman thoughtfully redirected us to an epic piece-of-crap location three marathon-long blocks away in a deserted alley behind a dumpster outside city limits. If he'd put us across the street from a maximum-security prison in Outer Mongolia, it wouldn't have been any worse than this. In fact, it would have been better; at least there would have been the occasional employee or paroled inmate to sell to.

I guess it shouldn't have mattered so much that our new location was possibly dangerous (definitely after dark) and pretty much totally invisible to pedestrians and the world. In all fairness to the officer, this alley and dumpster were sure to capture a few customers who had accidentally thrown something away the night before and would need to go looking for it, and for anyone who needed to commit a petty crime it was the perfect out-of-the way spot, and maybe a few people would sneak back here to take a leak on their way to Town Square, so we had that to look forward to.

Not to mention, how were we supposed to watch the cryogenic freezing while selling lemonade to rats and garbage men and forgetful people with a bad sense of direction? This was borderline police brutality, I suspected, but lacking a clear understanding of Montana law, and being hesitant to start a criminal record that would inevitably lead to a life of lawlessness, I decided to go with the flow and play along with the joker in the unitard and the laser-gun holster belt.

Throughout the entire ordeal, Mosquito barely managed to glance up from his Gameboy, showing absolutely no concern for the horrific turn of events, so when he said, "How about we leave everything here and go watch this guy get frozen to death already?" it really annoyed me. "We can't just leave all our stuff here," I said. "I invested five dollars in Wendy's signs, I arranged a credit line with Tilo's mom for the lemons, and I had to buy the sugar and the little drink umbrellas. We can't just abandon everything."

"But you said you already had the little drink umbrellas," Mosquito pointed out.

"Yes, I did, but I still had to buy them originally. So what if it was last summer or a billion summers ago? I still had to pay for them, they didn't just make themselves, and I've told you a thousand times that he's getting frozen to life, not death!"

"Can Tunafish pick us up?" Tilo asked.

I shook my head. "No, he's busy till later." When Tunafish dropped me off, he made extra sure to explain that if I needed a ride home, I would just have to wait until he was good and ready, because he wasn't planning to finish his nature hike until evening at the earliest. He loved to watch birds whistle sweet symphonies to each other while mountain goats and bobcats and grizzly bears pranced around playfully in a smorgasbord of imagery and a cacophony of sound so profound that Tunafish would inevitably be moved to tears. This very minute he was probably sitting on a rock by a stream, stark naked, crying his eyes out, marveling at the unfathomable beauty of it all.

So I carried the table, the tablecloth, a chair, and the moneybox. Tilo carried the lemons, another chair, and the pitchers, and Mosquito carried everything else, but not happily. It was only five and a half blocks from the alley to Tilo's house, so it wasn't exactly the Bataan Death March, but it was a depressing walk of shame. Our tails were tucked.

Ten minutes later we arrived at Tilo's house, dropped the lemonade paraphernalia in the garage, and turned right back around to watch the big chill go down.

8

Watching someone get frozen to death, or life, depending on how you look at it, while sipping a white chocolate grande frappuccino through a twisty straw is a wonderfully absurd and somewhat extravagant experience. I highly recommend it if the opportunity arises.

The sun was shining, a gentle breeze was blowing, the sweet smell of pansies and daisies wafted through the crisp mountain spring air. All the potential gunslingin' hullabaloo was being kept to a minimum by my good friend Mr. Policeman, who, from what I could tell, was just as annoyingly pedantic with everyone he encountered as he was with me. This was comforting to realize, a revelation, in a way, because I had interpreted our earlier encounter as a highly personal thing, a calculated slap in my face, when in fact it was par for the course for the pinhead country pig, business as usual. This was his thing, exercising minuscule amounts of authority over innocent unsuspecting upstanding taxpaying citizens like me. In a lot of ways the policeman was impersonating a robot, devoid of empathy or compassion and incapable of grasping the psychological nuances of complex social interactions. It felt good to understand this. It was water under the bridge. I was here to enjoy myself.

"Can you please rewind and pass the peanuts, Tilo, and turn up the music while you're at it," I said.

Tilo informed me that he didn't have a remote control for this event and thus wouldn't be able to "rewind or turn up the music, and I have no peanuts or popcorn to offer you, either."

"I was just kidding, Tilo. A little levity after Colonel Peacock's cold shower can't hurt."

"What? Did I miss it?" Mosquito grumbled. "Was that it? Is it really over? That's it? That was worse than a bris. A science fair is more exciting than that. What a waste of time!"

"A man's entire life just flashed before his eyes as he was preserved for eternity," I replied. "Show some respect."

Mosquito snorted. "It still broke the golden rule."

"What golden rule?"

"It was boring. One second it's say hi to the snooty, snotty, richer than Richie Rich Montgomery Peacock, and then yadda yadda yadda, and poof, he's frozen, that's it, show's over, don't forget to tip your waitress on your way out. I don't think so."

"So you felt it was overly hyped and anticlimactic?" I said.

"Bingo, how'd you guess? Oh, probably because you're the jerk who told me about it in the first place. I deserve an apology."

"You're right, I forgot to mention that cryofreezings are more of an internal experience that can seem dull to unimaginative and negatively inclined people. But never mind that, Mosquito, because your unconscious mind will be wrestling with this for years to come, I promise."

"Yeah, well, I'd rather clean my ears with your promises."

"You mean my promises are like Q-Tips?" I was confused.

"Ask me no questions, and I'll tell you no lies," he retorted.

"April showers bring May flowers," I replied.

"A bird in the hand is worth two in the bush," he shot back.

Tilo interrupted our poetic face-off. "Have you guys gone crazy?"

"They're called proverbs, Tilo. A proverb conveys an idea that is truthful, usually based on common sense, and if it's a really good proverb that everyone thinks is super insightful, it graduates to aphorism status, which is pretty much the highest honor there is for an expression, beats an adage any day, I would say, anything except for an epitaph, which should really be in its own category altogether."

"Who cares?" Tilo said.

"You should care, because the kindergarten kids and preschoolers of tomorrow depend on us for their lives, for the ultimate survival of the human race. The entire Planet Earth, for that matter, is in our hands. If we don't come up with a clever solution to the outlandish mess our predecessors have left us, our little friends in diapers won't have a planet to live on, or a tetherball court to play on. Nothing. Have you ever thought about that, Tilo?"

"I just saw a strange girl with curly hair walk into the pet store."

"So?" Mosquito said.

"So maybe we should go check out the pet store," Tilo said.

"Somaybeweshouldgocheckoutthepetstore," Mosquito parroted at fast-forward speed.

"You're so annoying, Vito,"

"My name is either Mosquito or Vito the Mosquito, never ever Vito all by itself. Comprende?"

"Yeah, I understand, Vito the Mosquito wants Tilo the Burrito to demonstrate the difference between a half nelson and a full nelson. Or would you rather learn the inverted three-quarter facelock with body scissors? It's your call, amigo."

Mosquito didn't respond, he just breathed and blinked a few times and then nodded his head ever so slightly up and down.

"Does that mean yes? Yes, you want to learn the nelsons, or the facelock with the body scissors? Which one? You no good sonofagun."

Mosquito shook his head again, this time side to side.

"Okay, have it your way," Tilo said, and then he slapped Mosquito on the cheek hard, like a girl would if she was mad enough to really let loose and get her hips and torso into it, which would generate a significantly stronger SmackDown than a standard stationary arm-and-hand slap. It was the difference between ping-pong and table tennis; one was for amateurs.

Without missing a beat, Mosquito retaliated with a table tennis slap to Tilo's right cheek.

"I tried to avoid this," Tilo said, "but now it's time to unleash my latest creation. I call it the double chicken-wing dragon-sleeper cloverleaf leglock. In other words, prepare to die."

With that Tilo kneed Mosquito in the balls, knocking him to the ground, grabbing him by his wrists, and flipping him into a Mexican surfboard, a truly remarkable sight to behold.

It was Tilo's signature closing move, but he'd rarely executed it this well. It was because of this move that Tilo thought he had a slight chance of becoming a professional wrestler one day, with his own line of sleeping bags and lunchboxes. But Mosquito wasn't just going to roll over and play dead, and the two continued to pounce on each other like a couple of pit-bull/poodle mixes fighting at the dog park daintily and viciously and pathetically all at once.

Professional wrestling, like rap music and reality shows, is a quintessentially American contribution to the world. Unfortunately, our list of regrettable contributions is much longer, some of the highlights including credit default swaps, country music, and nuclear bombs, and not necessarily in that order.

I left my two squabbling ducklings to their own devices and sauntered over to the pet store to check things out.

9

Kid walks into a pet store, classic scenario, happens a thousand times a day all over the world. But not like this, not like today. Today was different. Today was that one day in a million when your life changes in an instant, when everything you know gets turned inside out and upside down and round and round.

I had caught only the faintest glimpse of the magical creature in the back of the store, but I knew without question, as sure as half a loaf is better than none but not as good as a whole one, that I would never be the same. I was lost in thought, standing in the doorway of the pet store, slurping on a chocolate, peanut butter, and mint chip milkshake of emotions that was giving me a noncryogenic brain freeze.

I was so discombobulated by the sheer presence of this ethereal being that I nearly curled up in the corner of the pet store and wept. This apparition was clearly the banshee fantasy figment of my imagination come to life, otherwise known as my soul mate, aka partner in crime. A soul mate, for those who don't know, is someone with whom you have an immediate connection the first moment you meet, a connection so strong that you're drawn to them in a not necessarily romantic way you've never before imagined. As this connection develops over time, you experience a love so deep and strong and complex that you begin to doubt that you've ever truly loved anyone before. Your soul mate might not agree with everything you say or do, but your soul mate understands you and connects with you on every level, which brings a sense of peace and happiness when you're around them, and when you aren't, you're that much more aware of the existential harshness of life and how bonding with another creature in this way is the most significant and satisfying single thing you can experience as a human being.

Is it weird, then, to be confronted suddenly, when you least expect it, in the back of a run-down pet store, by your soul mate? No question, but not nearly as weird as discovering that your soul mate is a turtle. Which is absolutely ridiculous, of course, and makes no sense at all, yet it felt so right, so comfortable and natural and strangely familiar, that I could have projectile-vomited from the dizzying insanity of it. But I didn't. I just burped and walked toward the girl with the fusilli hair who was holding my turtle in her hand.

She was in the five-feet-tall neighborhood and sporting a striped summer dress and a wild and carefree head of brown curls, no doubt the same girl Tilo had seen. She was cute in a Pippi Longstocking/Keri Russell circa *Felicity* kind of way, with a thousand freckles to prove it, arranged on her face like celestial constellations. I could have stared for hours, making out shapes and patterns without the hassle of a telescope and the night sky.

This girl had no idea, of course, that the turtle in the palm of her hand was my soul mate, how could she? I had just discovered it myself only moments ago. I took a deep breath and said, "Is he your turtle?"

She ignored the question, instead responding with a statement of such obviousness it made me wonder. "I've never seen such a fantastic turtle before!" she said.

Duh! A rocket scientist she was not. "Would you mind if I hold him?" I extended my hand.

"Go ahead," she said, haphazardly slapping him over to me like he was an egg roll or a biscuit that needed buttering before it was eaten. I was appalled. She must be mad, bonkers, crazy, carelessly manhandling a helpless little turtle like this. PETA would have a field day with her.

I, on the other hand, safely cupped him in my palm, using the other hand as a protective shield on top of him, in the unlikely event of an earthquake triggering falling debris. It was crystal clear to everyone, mainly the girl and me, that he was undeniably my doppelgänger in disguise. Let there be no mistake about it. This was a guarantee, a given, one of life's few absolutes. It felt like I had come home after a grueling day at school to find freshly baked chocolate chip cookies in the oven and a tall glass of 2% milk in the fridge, with a *Scooby-Doo* marathon about to start on the Cartoon Network, and nothing feels better than that.

I had been reunited with my long-lost turtle at last, after hundreds, possibly thousands of years, and it felt so good that it cued the jukebox in my brain to play Peaches & Herb's classic hit *"Perfect Fit,"* and sugar this one was it.

"We both are so excited," she said.

"Because we're reunited," I said.

"Hey, hey," she said, and then, just as I had anticipated, she added, "and he kinda looks like you."

"Really?" I said, gushing with pride.

"Yeah, like he's your soul mate or something."

My heart nearly stopped beating. "What did you say?"

"I'm kidding. It was a joke, because he's a turtle and you're not and you guys don't look anything alike, obviously. I was being ironic. Sorry. If you were an animal, though, I would peg you as a platypus or a penguin, not a turtle."

"Why a platypus?" I said as nondefensively as possible.

"I don't know, that's what I see," she said, jabbing a knife in my heart.

Which provoked me to respond, "Well, you look like an antisocial yellow-bellied sapsucker, has anyone ever told you that?"

"If I didn't know you better, I might think you were talking smack," she said, "and since I don't know you, are you?"

"Not intentionally, no, it was more of a backhanded compliment. Yellow-bellied sapsuckers are quite beautiful, actually."

"Now that I think about it, you look a lot like a red-cocked woodpecker," she said. "It must be your eyes."

"Enough about birds," I said, "let's talk turtle."

"I don't know that much about turtles, except that they're reptiles and they can live for a long time. Probably longer than my grandpa will get to, frozen or not."

"Excuse me?" I said.

"You're excused," she said.

"No, did you say something about your grandpa being cryogenically frozen? Like Montgomery Peacock is your grandpa?"

"It's still a rather sensitive subject, if you don't mind."

Unable to contain my enthusiasm, I said, "Congratulations! Or my condolences, I guess it depends on how you look at it. So which is it?"

"Both. Thank you."

We avoided eye contact as a thick layer of awkwardness enveloped us like fog over the San Francisco airport in July.

"Can I have my turtle back?" she said.

What? Now my heart wasn't stopping, it was beating in triple quintuple time, as if Dave Brubeck himself was orchestrating my internal organs. Thankfully, my brain was equipped with a state-of-the-art rationalization app: she just wanted to hold him again, right? Don't panic, why wouldn't she? But I had to clarify.

"When you say 'can I have my turtle back,' what specifically do you mean by that exactly?"

"I mean can you kindly hand me the turtle so I can pay for him and go home and play with him. What else could I mean?"

Defeated. Demoralized. Devastated. I relinquished control over the turtle. "But you don't own him yet?" I asked.

"I basically own him. Possession is nine tenths of the law."

"Now you tell me."

"Tough luck, kid."

"But I need him. Please. I beg you! Let my turtle go."

"It was my grandpa who was frozen to death today, not yours. Emotionally speaking, I'm a delicate flower right now, and you're standing here haggling with me like I'm scalping Wu-Tang Clan tickets," she said with astonishing poise and clarity, like she moonlighted as a hostage negotiator for the Montana branch of the FBI Crisis Negotiation Unit.

I thought about grabbing the turtle and shoving him in my back pocket and running for the door, but knew I wouldn't get far before my old policeman buddy on the Segway caught up with me. I thought about screaming bloody murder and falling to the ground and flopping my arms and legs around and convulsing like a maniac having a seizure, creating such a ruckus that everyone got distracted enough that I could sneak out the back door with the turtle under my tee-shirt, but that was definitely not going to work, because everyone knows you can't be both the decoy and the escapee. So I did the only thing I could, which was fast becoming one of my signature moves. I dropped my head in defeat as a tear trickled down my cheek.

"Tough luck," she repeated. "My name's Daffodil. I just moved here from Missoula. My grandpa used to own the Peacock cattle ranch, and now my parents do, which is why we moved. What's your name?"

"Just call me the sorriest, saddest sack of potatoes in the world," I said, reaching a new level of self-pity.

"That's a really long nickname. Mind if I call you Sad Sack for short?"

"Sure," I said. "Why not."

"What could possibly be so sad?"

"Let's just say today was the second-worst day of my life."

"I'm sorry to hear that."

"I appreciate your condolences, but that doesn't help me. I want to take care of that turtle and feed him and become inseparable best pals with him for the rest of my life. It's a guy thing. You wouldn't understand. I don't even understand myself. It's not an intellectual thing, it's an instinctual thing. I can feel it in my bones and in my belly. That turtle is inexplicably inextricably connected with my destiny." I fell to my knees and put my hands together in prayer position, groveling. "So can I please have the turtle?" And with that, I rested my case.

Daffodil crossed her arms, shifted her weight from one foot to the other, and struck a pose while considering my plea, much like a jury of preteens would. She puckered her lips and looked me over from head to toe, then sighed dramatically.

"No way, Jose."

Despite her lighthearted choice of expressions, her tone was decisive and definitive, and she didn't seem to be particularly conflicted about the verdict either.

"I have a really nice aquarium," she went on, "and I just think he'll be happier with me, but it was nice to meet you. Hope to see you around." With that, she pocketed the turtle and glided away in her pink camouflage Heelys Sassy Roller Skate Shoes, yet again putting my soul mate in unnecessary peril. Why couldn't she hop, skip, or jump like a normal kid?

It's stupefying how the world works sometimes. Innocently enough, I was minding my own business, moderately coping with the meaninglessness of life, when I happened to walk into a pet store, on a whim and some bad advice (thank you, Tilo), and the next thing I know, I've fallen down a rabbit hole, with no idea which way is up (also a common experience when you're caught in an avalanche, in which case you're supposed to spit a loogie to see which direction it falls, but ideally you should avoid being in an avalanche). Then a strange siren of a girl utters one simple syllable consisting of two basic letters, N and O, and bang bang! my whole life comes crashing down. If only she had said those same two letters in reverse, if only she had said, "ON one condition, that you promise blah blah blah."

Why didn't she say that? It would have been just as easy, and it wouldn't have completely derailed my destiny, possibly altering irrevocably my monumentally important fate in the cosmos. It's always something.

Why-why? A question not to be confused with the infamous Chinese artist, pronounced "Way-Way," who was persecuted by the Chinese government, and who, like me, probably didn't know why-why things were the way-way they were. What was the point? Could somebody please give me a clue, a hint of some kind? Why couldn't I just have whatever I wanted whenever I wanted it? Was this my karma holding me back? Was I paying the piper for some previous life? Did I owe Julio money for something? Or was I just a pansy-asteroid snot-nosed kid, afraid to stand up for myself and what I believed in, equally afraid of success and failure, afraid of life and death, afraid to stop being afraid?

My self-loathing introspection came to an abrupt halt when I caught sight of the all too familiar copper sparkle I'd come to love so much. There was a penny on the floor by the display of dry cat food, next to a cardboard cutout of a calico kitty brushing up against a middle-aged male catalog model's left leg, its tail in the air, a smile on its face, probably because of all the money and free Friskies it was raking in for appearing in these ads. A sweet gig, no doubt. But then I wondered if that kitty cat got to spend its own money on catnip and fake mice, or if it had the typical domineering showbiz mother/manager/nightmare holding the purse strings and shouting out orders.

I walked over, desperate to make a wish, but when I bent down to pick the penny up, I saw the dreaded Lincoln Memorial, which meant tails, which meant no luck was to be found here, so I made a rash and unprecedented decision based on the theory that under these circumstances I was permitted a little leeway on the particulars of lucky-penny collecting. Dire straits called for dire measures, so I just went ahead and made a wish anyway! Why not? I needed to, there was nothing else to do, and it was the easiest, most rational and logical wish I ever made.

I closed my eyes and wished that I had never met that god-awful spaghetti head, Daffodil Peacock.

10

Being sucked into a supermassive black hole of despair isn't fun. I was trapped in the proverbial phantom zone of infinite space, just like General Zod and the rest of the Kryptonian criminals, floating in a purgatory of eternal loneliness without Pop-Tarts or Capri Suns. I was lost forever and ever in total silence and solitude with nowhere to go and nothing to do. Cold and shivering, lonely and lugubrious, put a fork in me, I was done.

Supermassive black holes are regions in the space-time continuum (also known as the sky, particularly at night) that exert such a strong gravitational pull that absolutely nothing at all can escape from them, nobody and no one, no meteors or planets or stars, not even the tiniest speck of light, not even your night-light in the hallway by the bathroom. Nothing. Like a big-shot Hollywood movie producer, a supermassive black hole consumes everything in its presence, sucks it up and spits it out.

Astrophysicists generally agree that there is probably a supermassive black hole in the center of every galaxy, and that this is precisely where our galaxy emerged from to begin with, and will probably return to in the end.

Other people believe that black holes are where you'll find wormholes and wormholes are the name of the game because they're shortcuts into other dimensions and universes, like a Midtown Tunnel through time or a Teleport Terminal to distant worlds.

Wormholes are more convenient than, say, the school bus for transport over impossible distances, they're cosmic superhighways with magnetic levitation trains, like in Shanghai, and no tolls or local stops to slow you down. The only problem, which is fairly inconvenient, is getting back in one piece. Return tickets are hard to find. Which isn't so different than it was for fifteenth-century explorers who set sail searching for adventure and riches with absolutely no idea what would happen or how, or who they would meet, or if they would ever return. That was what made it so exciting, I bet, the uncertainty, the mystery, the danger, the hunt for more clues to help unravel the mystery of our existence. That was what it was all about. Unless, of course, you were born into royalty or oil money, in which case you'd probably grow content eating grapes from the fingers of mermaids and actually start to enjoy the slapstick antics of the court jester, e.g., falling down and getting back up again, over and over.

Just my luck, I stepped off the school bus and into a puddle,

completely soaking my socks and shoes and my already dampened spirit. I
was thinking how symbolic of my entire existence this was when I walked
headfirst into the front door of the middle school. My god, what was wrong
with me, I could have sworn it was open, and then while I was hunched
over wiggling my nose around checking for blood and broken cartilage, the
door swung open fast and hit me on top of the head, hard enough to give
me a bump. Could life get any worse? Would this torture never end? Bad
luck had become my most pronounced quality. It was crazy how it worked:
the more good luck I wished for, the more bad luck I got.

I looked up at the sky and raised my arms and asked any pilots or
passengers or birds that might be flying by, "Why me?" Why was I flat
broke except for my penny collection? Why had I busted my nose and my
head? Why was I down in the dumps in a blue funk that smelled like a
skunk but looked like a monk trapped in the trunk? And why was I rhyming
at such an inopportune time?

I felt like that was a pretty good poem, not Walt Whitman caliber or
Shel Silverstein, but decent. I was impressed; it was cryptic applesauce,
yummy and delicious, I could eat it all day long. I should write it down and
one day self-publish a book of poetry on Amazon.com and get all the
elementary school students to buy it, and their parents, and their parents'
co-workers, and their co-workers' extended families, et cetera. If my poetry
was critically acclaimed, I could get a job writing for a Nickelodeon TV
show or the WB. Then I could drop out of middle school and travel the
world, maybe go to Prague or Paris or Portugal for some much needed R &
R, and when I came back to America, I'd be rejuvenated and ready to rock
and roll.

I'd probably decide to specialize in writing 3-D movies about animals
for kids. I would declare this as my specific area of concentration, my total
preoccupation and focus, my specialty, my "thing," if you will, and I would
hang a plaque on my door making it official so that when the big movie
studio CEO with the lucrative long-term contract from the chairman of the
parent multinational conglomerate (like Brad Grey, for instance) wanted to
make a 3-D movie about animals, he'd know exactly who to call. Me. It
would go something like this.

Brad, pacing back and forth in his plush Paramount Studios office,
suddenly yells to his secretary, Sally, "Quick, who can we get to rewrite that
Tim Burton jellyfish vampire movie we're doing in 3-D?"

His secretary shouts back, without missing a beat, "Willy Nilly's the man for the job, Mr. Grey, no question about it, because that's exactly what he does for a living, he writes animal movies in 3-D, that's his forte, his claim to fame, his pièce de résistance!"

"Then stop wasting my time with hyperbole and get him on the phone, already. My god, are we running a movie studio here or a nursery school!"

At which point the senior VP of development for Paramount would call and tell me how talented I was and how my words had changed the way people look at animated animals, and then offer to pay me a million bucks to rewrite the most commercially viable story about jellyfish vampires that had ever been done, and not to forget to rewrite it in three dimensions.

And all this success would stem from my laser-point focus in defining my niche from the get-go, immediately carving my persona in stone from the very beginning and not dillydallying with the myriad of different styles and genres and variations that don't pay the bills.

The key in a joust, and in life, is never to waver, not even for a moment, thus never allowing yourself even the slightest chance of not being pigeonholed. Because that's what we all really want, though we think we don't but act like we do, which is to be generalized or stereotyped and lumped in with others in an attempt to avoid the unbearable loneliness of being alone. And to succeed, all you have to do is follow one simple rule: write stories in three dimensions about animals. Or is that two rules? Mr. Dobalina would know.

Like the midday sun burning through the morning fog of a seaside village, my spirits began to lift a little at the thought of my favorite teacher and mentor imparting knowledge and wisdom to me. Teaching me the really important things about life: the English language, scientific things, philosophical things, anthropological things, and time permitting, the occasional get-rich-quick scheme.

The bell rang, prompting everyone to quickly squeeze into their little desk/chair combinations and pull out their sharpened Number 2 pencils, iPads, or smartphones so they could capture verbatim the thoughts of the great Dr. Dobalina (I'm guessing he has a PhD somewhere amongst all his achievements).

Because Mr. Dobalina was a super low-key humble guy who didn't dig the hype, a lot of people didn't know that for several years in a row he'd been the runner-up for *GQ* magazine's Coolest Guy in the Universe Award, but he never actually won, luckily. He told me he planned it that way. His hypothesis was that immediately upon winning the Coolest Guy in the Universe Award, you instantly were no longer the coolest guy in the universe because of the blatant obviousness of it. Therefore, the actual coolest guy in the universe was the official runner-up, making the official winner the actual runner-up. So Mr. Dobalina, intentionally, by default, was the coolest guy in the universe by virtue of being the second-coolest guy in the universe. Man oh man was he smart. Can you even imagine being able to comprehend the microscopic nuances involved in devising that kind of gumball slingshot theory? I hoped one day it would be me triumphantly losing the Coolest Guy in the Universe Award.

To prove his coolness to the class, but without trying, of course, Mr. Dobalina liked to cold-lamp in the old-school, Flavor Flav, Public Enemy style, not to be confused with the more literal meaning of cold lampin' (tapping into the electrical wires of a public street lamp to power DJ and MC equipment for purposes of hosting an aboveground underground hip-hop performance). Today Mr. Dobalina was luxuriously reclining, kicked back, feet in the air, in his special-issue, 94% recycled, ergonomically designed Herman Miller Aeron swivel chair, one of his few extravagant purchases after winning the prestigious Hugo Award last year.

Even more impressive than winning a Hugo Award (the highest honor for a science fiction or fantasy writer) was how Mr. Dobalina could eat a bag of salt-and-vinegar potato chips with a pair of plastic chopsticks while simultaneously sucking an Arnold Palmer through an elaborately constructed network of translucent straws stuck together like Legos in a complex network of interlocked tubes allowing Arnold to travel vast distances, from the desk, up and around, and back down into his mouth, without moving a muscle (not counting his cheek muscles, because they're hardly muscles). Talk about cool.

When the class was quiet, Mr. Dobalina removed the straw from his mouth and said, "I'd like to introduce you all to a very special, and I don't mean learning-disabled, young woman. Her name is Daffodil Abigail Peacock, and she will be joining our class today and every day after today, except on weekends and holidays, unless she wants to be here by herself, which she's perfectly welcome to do, but I won't be here and neither will you. Regardless, her legendary grandfather, as it happens, was a teacher of mine a long time ago, back at Howard University. As many of you know, he was cryogenically frozen on Saturday, but on Sunday, I'm sad to say, a maniacal raccoon on a rampage with a vengeance broke into the local power station and ate a transformer, temporarily taking down the entire town's electricity for six straight hours. Long story short, my old friend and Daffodil's grandpa defrosted and died yesterday. It's tragic, and I'm sure I speak for everyone, Daffodil, when I say that our deepest sympathies go out to you."

All of our heads and necks, but not our shoulders, turned in perfect unison to stare at the new student. She might as well have been an illegal alien from Guadalajara that just landed on the school lawn, because she did not seem one bit human, she seemed more like a giant praying mantis wearing a little-girl-with-curly-brown-hair Halloween costume.

The classroom was silent, except for the distinct but subtle sound of teardrops falling onto the linoleum floor. The fount of the tears, standing before the class, head drooped with sadness (like mine so often was these days), was the infamous turtle thief and newly bereaved granddaughter of the Peacock empire. She was crying so much there was a small puddle forming around her shoes. Plonk. Plonk. Plonk. And all the while, unknowingly, we were being sucked into a battle of wits. By appearing vulnerable and sympathetic she was trapping us in her web of destruction. She had us right where she wanted us. We were the ones who should have been crying, not her. And why wasn't she answering questions and telling us about herself? Was she really too sad? I was dubious, but I hated how callous I sounded, so I decided to pretend to be more sympathetic by sticking out my lower lip ever so slightly.

As I should have expected, the mind-blowing ingenuity of Mr. Dobalina came galloping to the rescue as he started crunching on his potato chips in rhythm with Daffodil's falling teardrops, adding a slurping effect from his intricate straw contraption to create a sexy afro-jazz beat that started my toe tapping. Daffodil Abigail Peacock, my oh my, you little minx. Herbie Hancock and Benny Goodman never sounded this good.

She utterly confused and inordinately saddened me. She was an unsolvable riddle, a contradiction of personality, a living, breathing, crying oxymoron come to life. I marveled at how extremely sympathetic she appeared when in fact she wasn't anywhere close. Like Martha Stewart, she could do no wrong, all the way to prison.

She wore her vulnerability like a Pop Swatch stuck to her sleeve, yet she was the very same girl who had heartlessly stolen my turtle out from under me. No one would have believed that this sweet little angel playing teardrops in an improvised jazz riff with the Bob Dobalina Jazz Quartet All-Stars had a horrifyingly heartless Frankenstein-like alter ego underneath, callously snapping up turtles left and right. Dr. Jeykll and Mr. Hyde had nothing on this double-dealing vixen from out of town.

Mr. Dobalina asked Daffodil to sit down so he could take center stage. It was his turn to entertain. The warm-up act was over, and now it was time for the main event, what we all were waiting for. Michael Jackson's "Thriller" started pumping from the Bang & Olufsen surround-sound system he had recently installed (at his own expense), and then the greatest educator of our time descended from the dropped ceiling on a hydraulic lift, surrounded by clouds of dense fog hovering over buckets of dry ice and illuminated by a simple spotlight that cast a cartoonish shadow of him on the chalkboard.

The iconic rock star/professor/philanthropist/poet grabbed the microphone. The class went wild, screaming and cheering and whistling. Mr. Dobalina remained frozen in a provocative pose while the roar of music and endless accolades faded and the smoke cleared. The prophet finally spoke, his words grumbly but confident and comforting; he could have been a baritone in a barbershop quartet.

"In the broadest sense, religion is a reference to the supernatural or the unexplainable. With the compilation of shapes and symbols arranged in a particular way, religions provide people with a set of ideas and belief systems about how and why the world exists, and most importantly, how to cope with misfortune."

Just then, punctuating "misfortune," the sound system cut out, firing off a few static ruffles and screeches before popping and hissing itself to death. Next the overhead spotlight exploded, draping the class in darkness and shards of glass and a long and awkward silence, as if we'd been put in a giant closet together for a humiliating game of Spin the Bottle and had all, in unison, admitted whose belly button we'd lick if we absolutely had to in a life-or-death situation.

And then the bell rang, which meant either that time had sped up while my perception of time had slowed down, or that class had been arbitrarily shortened today, or that Mr. Dobalina's electrical snafu had prematurely set off the bell, but I simply didn't have enough information to form an opinion, or even speculate about the bell's sheer existence in the first place.

11

From a distance Mosquito and I watched Daffodil play tetherball by herself on the asphalt courts of the playground under the noonday sun. She wasn't bad either. I was impressed, not that I would admit it to anyone; she had a strong swing, good dexterity, great balance, and an excellent attitude. She was formidable, no question about it.

And then, like a kick in the balls, I was zapped with a static shock of terror in the form of a painful self-realization: it was all too possible, bordering on likely, that Daffodil was better than me at tetherball. My god, please don't let that be true. Anything but that, please: Buddha, Jesus, Muhammad, Joseph, L. Ron, Flying Spaghetti Monster, whoever you are, I beg you! I'll do anything. All right, don't panic. Composure. Get a grip on yourself, Sergeant Major Willy Nilly. This was all still very theoretical, complete conjecture, unconfirmed gibberish, but my stomach sensed something bad.

The solution to my potential problem was staring me straight in the face: just don't play tetherball with her, at least not an actual game, for as long as you live, easy as that, problem solved, nothing to worry about.

Mosquito, pest that he was, changed all that when he screamed across the playground, "Hey, Daffodil, oh Daffodil, come out, come out, wherever you are."

Daffodil seemed to be in some type of tetherball trance, or else she was good at ignoring super loud and annoying kids yelling her name, but eventually she turned to see what all the ruckus was about.

Mosquito tried to signal to Daffodil, without yelling, that we---pointing first at me, then at her---should play a game of tetherball. While she was trying to decipher his confusing pantomime, the swinging tetherball smacked into her kisser like a drunken sailor. Little birdies circled and chirped appropriately. Then, with astonishing aplomb, dignified and unapologetic, she flipped her hair off her face, checked her nostrils for blood and mucus, and approached us.

This was what my supposed friend Mosquito said next. "Looks like you're a snazzy little tetherball dynamo, Daffodil, you probably have your own Olympic coach and everything. In which case, I propose an epic battle of the sexes, Billie Jean King style, so we can finally find out whether or not my man Willy Nilly can hang with the big girls. This isn't elementary school anymore. What do you say we set the record straight once and for all? Because I think Daffodil thinks that she would clean your clock with a tetherball, Willy. Don't hate the middleman."

"Excuse me," Daffodil interjected, "but I never thought any such thing. Although you're probably right, now that I do think about it. Willy wouldn't stand a chance, no offense, and neither would you, Mosquito---is that why they call you Mosquito?"

"Huh?" Mosquito was quick to respond.

"Because you're annoying."

"I think I know where you're going with this, Ms. Peacock, and I don't like your tone, because nothing would please me more than to blindfold myself and put a straitjacket on and let you serve first, trust me, but unfortunately I'm a little under the weather today," Mosquito said, checking his forehead for a fever. "Plus I'm stuffed, all puckered out, I had a huge lunch and two desserts, the brownie and the key lime pie, both delicious. Anyway, Willy doesn't really have an A game, more of a solid B game, so if you can beat him, then you deserve a shot at the title, which would be against me, on another day. Let's just say that they don't call me the playground champ for nothing, if you catch my drift." To emphasize his point, Mosquito shuffled his feet clumsily, shadowboxing while doing his best Will Smith imitation of a Muhammad Ali imitation. "Because I float like a butterfly and sting like a bee."

Daffodil redirected her attention to me. "Are you ready to play some tetherball, Willy, or does your tummy hurt too?"

I stared at Mosquito with contempt. I shook my head in disgust and mouthed the words, "Were you dropped on your head as a baby?"

He smiled devilishly.

At this point I had no choice whatsoever but to play the new girl. If I didn't, I was the Cowardly Lion, without any courage, but if I did, I was the dumb Scarecrow, without any brains. It was a trap, she was Dorothy and I was screwed, I couldn't win, I was checkmated, shipwrecked, and all out of tokens, with nowhere to run and nowhere to hide. I'd been triple-jumped on the checkerboard by my own imbecilic friend, through no real skill of his own, just dumb luck and chutzpah.

Game theory, as Mr. Dobalina so eloquently explained on the first day of school, is the study of strategic decision-making between intelligent and rational people, but Vito the Mosquito was most certainly not rational. He was a live wire, a loose cannon, maybe even a sociopath, I couldn't be sure.

I took a sliver of comfort from the fact that I had no choice in the matter, strategically speaking, as a student of game theory. I had to play Daffodil, honor before all else, never mind that I shouldn't be held accountable for a sneak attack by some crackerjack calling himself my friend while forcing me to defend my reputation, not only as a tetherball player, but as a man! I think they call it coming to terms with the inevitable. So I decided to pretend I was a Roman gladiator, ready to fight ferociously to my death defending my honor at all costs, whatever it took. Wind me up and let me go, I could do this.

Graciously, Daffodil offered to let me serve first. I graciously accepted. Violently smacking the ball with the palm of my hand, I served with everything I had. It whizzed by her head, once, twice, almost three times before she skillfully hopped up like a volleyball player spiking the kill shot, returning the tether twice as hard in a confusing elliptical orbit around the pole. This threw me long enough to allow the tetherball to twist around the pole three times, then four, five, and bingo, touchdown, ding-dong, the fat lady had sung. Daffodil had won. I had lost.

Mosquito nearly died from laughter. He looked like a kid on a roller coaster having a seizure and a sneezing fit at the same time. I nearly died from embarrassment, and Daffodil nearly died from unmitigated satisfaction bordering on pure glee.

Naturally, I needed to rebound from this debacle as quickly as possible. "Were we playing two out of three or three out of five?" I asked innocently.

"I thought we were playing one game," she said, even more innocently. She was a tiger.

"No, of course not, it's never just one game. Who ever heard of best out of one? Plus, I'm sure you wouldn't want to win a match on one lucky block like that. Someone might call it a fluke or a once-in-a-million freak occurrence," I said with a straight face. "However, now that I understand your unconventional playing style, I'm confident I can beat you. Easily, "I taunted, without any basis for taunting.

Mosquito had recovered from his laughing fit just enough to chime in on my behalf, good friend that he was, "Come on, Daffodil, give the poor guy another chance. The wind was in your favor, and you took advantage of little Willy."

"I didn't feel any wind. Did you?" she asked me.

I shrugged my shoulders.

"Okay, fine, if you want another game, we'll play best out of three, unless you'd rather play best out of seven, or we could make it best out of seventeen or seventy-seven or seven hundred and seventy-seven, or best out of seven thousand seven hundred and seventy-seven, to make sure it's fair. It's your call, tough guy."

"Best out of three works for me," I said, rhyming for intimidation purposes. "It's your serve this time, porcupine."

I gave her the ball. She grabbed it, squeezed it, and spun it on her finger like a Harlem Globetrotter.

"Wait," I said, stepping off the court. "I need a moment to mentally prepare."

I closed my eyes and imagined that I was a tenth-century samurai warrior in a white forest of Japanese cherry blossom trees, defending a baby emperor from a thousand ninjas (Daffodil was the thousand ninjas and the emperor was the tetherball). I decided to play as unscrupulously as necessary to win, remembering, of course, that it was only tetherball at the end of the day.

Daffodil served a doozy to start the game. It swung right by me several times before I managed, just barely, to catch it with my left hand. We volleyed back and forth for a while. We were equally matched this time, I was holding my own, occasionally slipping in some sneaky stuff. Technically, my violations would have included multiple ropeys, a couple of crossies, and a double touchie, but there was no referee. For a spectator, I think it must have been an oddly entertaining concoction: one part vicious savagery (me), one part renegade lawlessness (me), one part sophistication (her) and another part grace (her), with a sprinkling of spastic displays of athleticism (me again). I ended up losing the game, big surprise, but it was a lot closer this time, and it left me with the fleeting fantasy that just maybe, under ideal circumstances, if the seas parted, I could beat her.

"I have an idea," I said. "How about we just make it best out of five and call it a day?" Daffodil didn't respond, so I explained. "That way it's a regulation match. Official rules, no asterisks in the record books. Plus, I feel like I'm just getting warmed up."

"No thanks."

"Come on, just one more."

"I guess no one ever taught you to leave the casino when you're ahead."

"But I'm not ahead."

"Exactly."

"So you admit it was luck?"

"I admit no such thing. You can try again tomorrow, peasant boy, but I'm done for today."

If she walked away now, I was a dead man. I wouldn't last five seconds before Mosquito crucified me, and then the entire school. My eyes would bleed and my ears would cry and I would burn in eternal middle school damnation. I was getting carried away, but then again, you never know what can happen on any given Sunday, Monday, or Tuesday.

With the tiniest bit of good luck on my side for once---a gentle breeze in my direction, a ray of sunlight in her eye---I could take her downtown, all the way to Loser Street. I had absolutely no choice but to think this way. I was in survival mode. I had to double down and go for broke, so I said, "Here's the thing, Daffodil. I was peacefully minding my own affairs a few minutes ago, over there, you remember, while you were over here methodically practicing the professional tetherball moves you've managed to acquire at such a young age. Well, I won't bore you with all the details, but now that I'm finally ready to play, and I mean really ready, ready-ready, all you want to do is quit. Which poses the question, is she a one hit wonder, flash in the pan, fly-by-night, two-bit tetherball hustler?"

"That's pretty good. Did you just make that up?"

I held my right index finger in the air.

"Gesundheit," Daffodil said.

"What? I didn't sneeze."

"Did you fart?"

"No. Why, does it smell?"

"No, you held up your finger like you had to sneeze or fart."

"I was just visually reinforcing my humble request for one more chance." I started to swing my right arm around in circles, like a traffic cop or a third-base manager directing his runner home. Then I stopped swinging my arm and started wiggling my fingers on both hands, limbering them up so I didn't jam one (a common tetherball injury), but it easily could have seemed like I was trying to cast a spell on Daffodil, which I was.

"Look," I said, "you're already up two games to zero, which means you're only one measly game away from becoming the world heavyweight champion---officially, I mean, as opposed to speculatively, based on an unofficial, rather casual, nonchalant, barely-even-keeping-score, just-for-fun match kind of thing. Unless, of course, you're afraid your luck's finally run out, in which case, I understand."

"You really are a masochist," she said. "I was trying to cut you a break, but if you insist, then fine. I'm willing to play best of five, on one condition. We make it more interesting for me, if you catch my drift."

Being a man of not great wealth, I pretended to misunderstand. "More interesting?"

"I'm suggesting a simple wager, Willy. If I win, which of course I will, you'll have to be my personal assistant for thirty days."

I was born to negotiate, even without fully understanding the proposition. "Twenty-eight!" I said.

"Thirty-two," she shot back.

"Fine, make it thirty," I said. "What does a personal assistant do, anyway?"

"Whatever I want. You'd be my little helper elf, my butler, my gofer, my attendant, my go-between, my subordinate, my servant, my lackey, valet, yes-man, bird dog, my umbrella holder---you want me to keep going?"

"Nope, I get it, you want me to be your bitch. But what about me? What do I win if I win?"

"I prefer the term 'personal assistant,' or 'executive assistant,' or any of the options I just threw out, and if you win---and honestly, the chances are so low it doesn't matter, but if it makes you feel better, if you win the next three games I'll be the best personal assistant you ever had."

"Is that what you think of me? That I'm a total loser, incapable of beating you? Fine. Then you won't mind if we play for the turtle instead."

"The turtle is out of the question."

"So you're all talk."

"No, you're all talk. I just don't gamble with other people's lives."

"We both know that anyone can get lucky now and then, happens all the time, which is why it's best-out-of-five matches that make champions. There's a reason nobody counts best-out-of-three matches, Daffodil, it's not a coincidence, it's because they're too susceptible to the accidental freak occurrence, which is exactly what happened today."

"My god, will you just stop talking? You want the turtle, I get that, and

I want a subordinate. So fine, you beat me the next three games in a row, turtle's yours, but when I win, you work for me for free for a month and you do whatever I want, no matter what, no excuses, got it?"

"Got it," I said.

"Only solutions," she said. "I serve first."

"Go right ahead," I said.

Daffodil grabbed the ball with more intestinal fortitude than previously displayed. It scared me. She took a deep breath and closed her eyes, probably to mentally visualize herself winning in heroic fashion, a trick she'd no doubt learned from watching me, or maybe she really did have an Olympic tetherball coach. As she stood there with her eyes closed, head high, back straight, it was obvious that she was no amateur. She was the Black Widow of tetherball, which made me the Minnesota Fats, I guess, which raised the question, how come no one has made an iconic film about tetherball hustlers?

The stage was set. You could cut the tension in the air with a Number 2 pencil and a protractor. Despite the fact that I had decisively lost both previous games, I still wasn't convinced. She was beatable. Everyone is.

I took a deep breath and reminded myself that I had no choice but to win. Everything was on the line. My entire life had led to this moment, the proverbial fork in the road: one way went toward reclaiming my dignity and my turtle, and the other way went the other way.

I asked Mosquito to slap me in the face, "but not too hard," I said. "Hard enough to give me a quick reality check, but not so hard that you break my neck, capiche?"

Like a jilted lover, Mosquito wound up and slapped me as hard as he could, with a smack that reverberated across the playground. Daffodil winced. The Coney Island Polar Bear Club, the oldest winter bathing organization in the United States, believes a quick dip in freezing water is the best way to revive your senses and cleanse your soul; the same can be said for a good slap in the face, although the bright red tattoo of a hand on your cheek is never a good look.

Daffodil raised the ball as if to say, "Look closely, Mr. Nilly, this will be the death of you." Then she juggled it back and forth as if she was revving her engine and getting ready to peel out, and then she twisted her hips, bent her knees, and cranked her right arm back so far it looked like she was the genetically enhanced offspring of a Polynesian contortionist and an Olympic discus champion, and then the tetherball blasted from her fingers like a cannonball, with a ferocious ferocity and a cosmic sense of purpose that was undeniably awe-inspiring. It turned out to be what is affectionately known in the sport of tetherball as a cherry bomb, where the server wins the game before the opponent is able to get even one of his greasy paws on the ball.

It's fair to say, and the local papers and Mosquito's personal blog surely will, that I was destroyed and humiliated in epic fashion by the new girl, in what many are calling the Fight of the Century, with Ms. Peacock as Joe Frazier, and me, of course, as Muhammad Ali, iconic athlete, mighty fine poet, and shining symbol of the anti-establishment movement, now sadly suffering his first professional loss to Daffodil, symbolizing the conservative, pro-war, pro-Wall Street Prozac nation. It was a sad day for America.

Make no mistake about it, this was an unambiguous horror show. There was no way to spin it, flip it, hide it, ignore it, reposition it, deny it, and there was no way around it. Famed public relations agency Rogers and Cowan could have built a gold-plated skyscraper with the fees it would cost to make this debacle disappear. I had been annihilated in every way: mentally, physically, and spiritually. I wanted to cry, but that would only have added insult to injury, the compound fracture of my ego.

Desperate times called for desperate measures, so I did what anyone would have done in my position. I pretended I had to pee. I hunched over and knocked my knees together and rocked back and forth and made a series of contorted faces while spastically pointing at my zipper and biting my lower lip to convey the urgency of how badly I needed to get out of there.

This was no time for a Golden Globe or an Emmy, I needed to deliver an Academy Award-winning performance or be forever remembered not only as a total tetherball turkey but also as a pansy-ass pee-pee faker who couldn't take the pressure and went hopping for the hills. I used Marty the Zebra from the hit *Madagascar* film franchise as the inspiration for my style of improvisational hop/skip/sashay/shuffle/prance flight from the scene of a crime. It was appropriately eccentric and erratic and bizarre, a desperate bid to temporarily distract everyone from the issue at hand.

Soon I was halfway to paradise, safely away from the playground, nearly inside the school, where I could hide, and then I spotted a penny on the grass. On closer inspection its tail was up, of course. What should I have expected? I had grown to loathe the Lincoln Memorial.

12

A long time ago Japanese samurai warriors would commit hara-kiri (pronounced Harry Kerry) rather than be captured alive by an enemy clan of ninjas and risk the chance of being shamed, tortured, or embarrassed to death. For those of you who don't already know, I'm sorry to be the one to break the bad news, but if I don't tell you, someone less amiable probably will: hara-kiri is the ceremonial self-disembowelment of a samurai warrior. Sometimes performed in front of spectators, the ritual consists of writing a short death poem (usually a haiku or a limerick, but occasionally, under extreme circumstances, magnetic refrigerator poetry has been used with good results) that is read aloud, directly followed by plunging a dagger or a sword into your belly, like a fisherman gutting a mackerel, and when you've ripped out your intestines and thrown them in the trash, you put your head on a block of wood, stretching your neck kindly, so your executive assistant can chop it off for you.

For reasons I will never understand, hari-kari was the preferred method of restoring the honor of a mighty warrior, but it seems rather extreme and permanent, even for losing a tetherball match to a girl. If I'd been part of the Fujiwara clan in twelfth-century Japan, without Pop-Tarts or Capri Suns to cheer me up, I might have felt differently. And who am I to judge, anyway? Although I do feel I possess many of the same qualities you would hope to find in a Supreme Court justice, or at least a top TV judge like Joe Brown or Judge Judy. For example, if I make it a point to stay focused, I can maintain terrific eye contact, with a minimal amount of blinking, for extended periods of time, and I have no hidden agendas or dirty secrets or dirty laundry---I don't even change my socks, it's all out in the open, blowing in the wind. In fact, I often feel like I'm the most objective and reasonable, and if I'm being totally honest with you, the most intelligent person in the world, period, but my uncle Tunafish told me everyone thinks that---not about me, about themselves.

I couldn't tell if it was the morning dose of sodium amytal pills my mom gives me or the Oliver Stone marathon movie weekend on TNT or the beginnings of a nervous breakdown, but I was getting the sneaking suspicion that my lucky penny collection was failing me, and maybe even conspiring against me. It seemed increasingly obvious that whatever I wished for I was guaranteed not to get. I don't mean to suggest that whatever I *didn't* wish for I *did* get, no, that wasn't how it was working either. It just wasn't working. My *un*lucky penny collection had brought me nothing but empty promises from me to myself---the worst kind---and a heaping pile of worthless zinc that was bankrupting America to boot. It had to stop. There was no point to collecting pennies, clearly, because there was no point to existence at all. Apparently human beings were just accidental products of random evolutionary processes in a universe that was itself without purpose or meaning, which made collecting pennies particularly worthless.

Why had I stepped in a puddle and banged my nose? Bad luck? Nope, because I wasn't paying attention. Why was I humiliated on the playground and turned into a personal assistant? Bad luck? Nope, because I'm a crappy tetherball player with a big ego. Why did I sit on bubble gum in the school bus and get it all over my pants? Again, not paying attention. I'm a klutz. Will I ever learn? Probably not. Luck is for morons. Buddha and my mom were right. Shoot.

Wow, I hated my pennies! I'd fight them if I could. It was hard to imagine a more unruly, unreliable, and unlucky bunch of pennies than my lot of losers. Enough was enough. I was no longer entertained by the sheer notion of wish making; the act of wishing simply wasn't satisfying anymore without the wish occasionally coming true. I needed some reciprocity, some tender loving care and attention in return. Bottom line, I needed results I wasn't getting. I couldn't show these numbers to my board of directors; if I had one, they would fire me for incompetence. A boy can only twiddle his thumbs for so long. If I was an ostrich, I would bury my head in the sand, but since that was a common fallacy about ostriches and I wasn't one, I planned instead to Harry Kerry my super-duper worthless unlucky penny collection to death. Not by stabbing it repeatedly in the abdomen and chopping its head off, fun as that sounds, but it wouldn't work on a glass barrel filled with coins. No, I would bury them in my backyard, ceremonially, like my father was buried at his funeral. To do this right I needed a coffin and a cardboard tombstone that said something bold and definitive, like *Shit out of luck*. My mom would hate that, but she would never see it, and this was no time for censorship. It was time for redemption. I had lived in the unlucky shadow of my dead old man for too long.

I got a shovel from the barn and headed for the perfect spot to dig the grave. It was about a six-minute pogo-stick hop away, under four minutes if you walked. The winding dirt path, lined with bushes and trees, went up steeply at first, leveling off and then around and back down the other side of the hill, at the base of which were half a dozen humongous rocks, arranged in a curious formation that gave them the undeniable appearance of being a distant cousin twice removed to Stonehenge.

There were a few blackberry bushes here and there, as well as some ponderosa pine trees and firs and elms, and a quaint baby pond that was more like an overly confident puddle, but picturesque just the same. It made the whole setting work, unifying what might have otherwise been an incongruous and discombobulated backdrop. Gustav Klimt would have been delighted to rest his easel here and paint a geometric abstract landscape that would one day, after he had kicked the bucket and couldn't spend it, sell for a hundred million or more.

My massive glass penny jar was too heavy to carry, so I had to load it onto my wagon for transport. If I had to guess, conservatively speaking, I'd say it held close to ten thousand pennies, but I couldn't know for sure. All I knew was that it looked like a bank vault in the shape of a pickle barrel, as tall as me (four and a half feet) and wide enough to fit a baby giraffe in.

It turned out that getting my pennies onto my rusty Radio Flyer was the easy part. It was the tugging, lugging, towing, pulling, schlepping, dragging, and yanking that nearly killed me. My secluded burial oasis was much less convenient than I had anticipated. If I hadn't already dug the grave, I would have relocated it somewhere closer. It took every last ounce of strength I had just to get the wagon up and over the meandering pathway, but I made it. And I was pleased that neither my mom nor my uncle had caught sight of what I was doing. It's never easy to explain these types of things.

I aligned the Radio Flyer so all I had to do was tip the enormous vat of pennies out of the wagon and into the grave. The glass cracked as it crashed into the dirt hole. I didn't care. Those pennies were ancient history to me. Yesterday's news. A sad and distant memory already. I decided to say a few words in loving memory of my once cherished and now despised collection of unlucky pennies. I mumbled through most of it, since no one was listening, and then I said some stuff about the loss of innocence and trading my naiveté in for a new bicycle or a rickshaw or a Segway one day when I could afford it.

I filled the grave with dirt and squirted a few drops of Capri Sun over it as a symbol of the solidarity we never had, and for the homies I never had, except for the Homies I collect, two-inch action figures depicting realistic-looking Southern California Mexican Americans, aka Chicanos, in realistic situations, often as gang members or bank robbers or any type of mustachioed hoodlum. Eventually, after a backlash from the PTA and the LAPD arguing that they glorified gang life, the Homies were given elaborate new back stories highlighting the positive sides of their personalities. Most of them were now living exemplary lives as paroled prisoners, spending all their time doing charity work for the betterment of the community and teaching kids to stay in school and out of jail.

I wasn't sentimental generally, but as I thought about all my incredible wishes that had never come true, I felt a pain in my heart like a charley horse in my leg that Pepto-Bismol couldn't cure. Holographic representations of my dreams, like steam rising from a manhole, started to waft up from the grave like ghosts, hovering momentarily only to be sucked away a second later into eternal oblivion. I watched with awe and regret for what never was but should have been. It was a melancholic but intensely cathartic experience in Technocolor 3-D with digital surround sound. Some popcorn, Twizzlers, and a Cherry Coke would have been ideal.

My eyes started to well up. I wasn't sure if it was a freak case of spontaneous allergies or I was really sad and missed my dad, but thank god I was alone, this could so easily be taken out of context. I looked around, wide-eyed and paranoid, just to make sure. Then it happened. A hairline fracture in the Hoover Dam of my heart allowed a single tear to trickle down my cheek to the corner of my mouth, where my tongue was waiting. It was bittersweet, of course, how else can tears taste?

Watching my hopes and dreams disappear was like watching an original Shakespeare manuscript blow away before ever being read or misunderstood by anyone. It was a tragedy of epic proportions. I was lost and alone, wandering in the endless oblivion of nothingness, and I don't mean the Bumpkiville public library, I mean life.

Without dreams, without imagination, life would be brutally and unbearably boring and mechanical and pointless and intolerable. Which means, I think, that the entire point of existence is directly tied to the imagination. So why isn't there a definitive imagination operation manual with pictures, like from IKEA? Personally, I'd like to know how we're supposed to determine which of the millions of dreams and ideas that come into our head are the really important ones that need to be pursued at all costs. And how exactly do you turn ideas into actual living, breathing, tangible creations that can interact with other people's wild and crazy ideas, crashing and colliding and inspiring new hybrid half-breed dream mutations that propel humanity toward intergalactic harmony and a revelatory understanding of the paradoxical conundrum we call life?

One thing had become painfully obvious. None of these questions could be answered by collecting pennies.

13

I slept like a baby that night, which is not to say I slept sporadically, in fits and starts, like babies do; on the contrary, I slept soundly and steadily and dreamed wildly, like never before. I was flying over the North Pole in my Underoos, with a green cape draped around my shoulders and a giant C embroidered on my chest like I was Cucumber Man. But the weird part was how warm I was considering I was flying over the Arctic tundra in my underwear. It didn't make any sense. I wasn't even chilly. In fact, I was as hot as an egg in a sauna in Savannah in the summer. I was ready to burst and on top of the world. I was a pterodactyl who could dive and soar and do loopty-loos and shoot fire from my mouth and melt the ice caps faster than a Republican Congress. I was the man.

I had some difficulty with landings and takeoffs at first, but I got the hang of it fast and I was flying high. I was an ace fighter pilot extraordinaire without a plane. I flew bareback, old school, without a saddle or even a horse, just my arms and my legs and my fingers and toes. If I was tall enough and old enough to fly a plane, I would have been recognized for bravery, mostly because of that one time I flew in low along the coast at night, in the fog, under the radar, and single-handedly saved thousands of American POWs, mostly women and children, who were completely surrounded by enemy gunfire, with booby traps and trapdoors everywhere. How I managed to get them all safely into the plane and home, where a ticker-tape parade was waiting for us, along with a Purple Heart (from the president for my courage under fire), I will never know.

I was having the time of my life zooming around like Superman when suddenly a giant polar bear monster with a jet pack strapped to its back eyeballed me and started tailing me tight. I tried to shake him to no avail. I was fast, but he was faster. I was like Gene Hackman in *The French Connection*. It was hard to get a good look at the bear given our breakneck speeds, but I could clearly see that he had braces and blue teeth and what looked like a lobster bib around his neck---to keep his pearly white, dry-clean-only, cashmere-like fur from getting splattered with my blood and guts when he ate me like a rack of Applebee's delicious baby back ribs. It's not that I'm scared to die so much as I'm scared to be torn limb from limb and eaten alive by a polar bear. It's the practical things that frighten me. How, inevitably, little parts of me---my elbow, or my nostril, or my big toe--

-would get stuck between his teeth, and the other parts would get burped up and pooped out. But why do I care how I die? If I die I'll be dead, so it doesn't matter. Or does it? And why isn't being eaten alive by an overgrown, impetuous (he didn't even know my name) polar bear an honorable way to die? In some religions it probably is.

My alarm clock saved my life just in time. I brushed my teeth, combed my hair, and ate a frosted cherry Pop-Tart that my mom had lovingly toasted and buttered, in return for which I planted a smooch on her cheek on my way out the door.

A storm was brewing, I could smell it, so I shot my umbrella open like a spring-loaded snake out of a can of fake peanuts. Holding my umbrella quickly reminded me that I would soon be holding Daffodil's umbrella. She was the new boss, my CEO, the big cheese, which meant she was also my nemesis, because I couldn't be tamed. I wondered what exactly she had in mind for me. I hoped it wasn't inhumane, I didn't want to drag UNICEF into this, or the WTO or the Yes Men---god forbid. But one month wasn't the end of the world, and it had already started two days ago, technically. The clock was ticking, ticktock, ticktock, I hoped she realized that.

I gave myself an impromptu pep talk, slapping my cheeks like I was both the coach and the star player. I told myself that no matter what, I would stick it out till the bitter end, through thick and thin, health and sickness, better or worse, death do me part, so help me, O Pink Invisible Unicorn. I would fulfill my obligation to Daffodil, plain and simple, no excuses, under any scenario, and in the course of doing so I would regain my honor and self-esteem, so cruelly taken from me on the tetherball court that dreadful day.

I waited alone on a barren country road, sack lunch in one hand---also lovingly prepared by my mother---umbrella in the other. A few rickety mailboxes were barely holding on by a rusty nail and a prayer. A few feet away there was a crooked stop sign with seventeen bullet holes in it. The surrounding fields and forests were lush with colors, lots of yellows and greens in a myriad of obscure shades that aren't even found in a Crayola Super Pack. The storm was gaining momentum. The wind was fierce, unsympathetic, virile. It blew erratically, in all directions. I clung to my umbrella for dear life as raindrops the size of jelly beans began to fall from the sky and bounce off the ground like grasshoppers in a minefield of mousetraps. The clouds sneered, snickered, and snarled; I smiled back tauntingly. In the distance, my yellow school bus rounded the corner, starting the two-minute countdown till it arrived at my feet, ticktock, ticktock. A bus driver's second responsibility after safety is punctuality, because anyone can drive a bus but only the great ones can be on time all the time, ask a FedEx employee. My bus driver, apparently, was not one of the greats.

When I finally got to school I could smell trouble from the first moment I stepped foot through the front door. Taped to my locker, like *The Scarlet Letter*, for everyone in the school and the surrounding neighborhood and bordering counties to see, was a note, more like an execution sentence. It was fair to say this was the kiss of death for the social life I had one day hoped to cultivate. That dream was over.

Attention: William Nilliam of the 6th grade
This is Daffodil Peacock's to-do list. Which really means it's
Willy's to-do list for what Daffodil wants done.
Please note that the following items are not listed alphabetically,
or in order of priority, merely in the order in which I was able to
recall them while writing this note.
1. Feed my turtle.
2. Clean my turtle tank.
3. Play with my turtle and/or take him for a walk, and if possible,
make him laugh, or at least chuckle.
4. Carry my books if required.
5. Shine my shoes if requested.
6. Spritz my face if I ask or you notice that my skin looks parched.
7. Bottle my tears if or when I cry.
8. File patents for the following inventions: teardrop catcher,
Velcro fanny purse, new Magic Eye unicorn pattern (a Magic Eye
is an autostereogram that allows the viewer to see 3-D images by
focusing on 2-D patterns, thus engaging him or her to divert his
or her eyes from the obvious in order to see the hidden three-
dimensional image within).
9. Read to me from James Joyce's masterpiece *Finnegans Wake* as I
fall asleep at night.
10. Wake me up in the morning by reading *Finnegans Wake*.

I was floored. Completely dumbfounded. I stood there, mouth agape, pondering this preposterous note, my eyes glazed over like two delicious Krispy Kreme doughnuts. On the one hand Daffodil was basically handing over they keys to her turtle, which meant that my brother from another mother and I could hang out to our heart's content. An unusual stroke of good luck, I had to admit, but on the other hand Daffodil was insane. Apparently she had lost every marble in her collection. William Nilliam, my god! How did she ever come up with that? Spritz her face, file patents, read *Finnegans Wake*---I don't think so, I've tried! I crumpled up the to-do list, pretending as I did that I was the strongest man in the universe, three years running, with titanium claws for hands, capable of crushing anything, from diamonds to indestructible safety-sealed plastic packaging, effortlessly. The more I thought about it the more I realized how inappropriate Daffodil's humdrum list of hogwash was---I mean, posted on my locker door in broad daylight, for everyone to see? Was she for real? This bordered on psychological abuse, and if not, then libel or defamation or denigration, certainly vilification; I knew that Bert Fields (a reputable Hollywood lawyer) would think of something.

How she managed to scribble and squeeze so much nonsense into one single note, I will never know. And to assume that I would do it all like I was a modern robot-butler or an eighties child actor was absolutely maddening! The nerve. My god. So I lost one little tetherball match, shoot me, it happens. David Beckham didn't score a goal every time he kicked the ball; in fact, he rarely scored.

I could live with being her personal assistant, don't get me wrong. I wasn't scared, although I preferred executive assistant, but that was just semantics. I had come to terms with the concept, more or less, and like everything else in life, it was only temporary. Visionaries like P. Diddy's umbrella holder Farnsworth Bentley had paved the road for a respectable and dignified career as an executive assistant, proving yet again that it all depends on your point of view. Or take Dwayne Wade. There's obviously no shame in tossing an alley-oop to the best basketball player in the world. They call that an assist. What about handing a heart surgeon a scalpel? Even making Michael Bay his special iced double-decaf-half-caf soy macchiato with a twist of lemon and a sprinkle of cinnamon every day has its cachet.

Be that as it may, I couldn't let Daffodil just gallop into town on her high horse and expensive saddle, with matching boots, riding pants, helmet, and suede jacket, and lasso me like a cheap donkey and herd me off to Mozambique. She was just the new girl who caught a break and was looking to exploit the situation. I couldn't blame her for that, I might have done the same thing, but I certainly couldn't aid and abet her.

Reading her to sleep was one thing, but waking her up by reading the same book was total lunacy, laughable and logistically impossible. I had to put my foot down on this one or risk being walked on like hot coals at an ashram. I knew her type. She was a sheep in wolf's clothing, a sweet, innocent, adorable little unicorn on the outside and a diabolical devil inside.

Secretly, I admit, I somewhat admired her to-do list for its sheer audacity and inventiveness, and to be forced to spend time with "her" turtle was a dream come true, but I also greatly resented the patronizing tone of the entire note. It's a style thing, no finesse, no tact, no respect. How could she assume I didn't know what a Magic Eye was? I mean, for crying out loud, of course I know what a Magic Eye is, everyone knows! I've even been working on my own uniquely patentable Magic Eye pattern for years, she's not the only one. Her presumptuousness was profound.

After burying my pennies, I had undergone an intense psychological makeover, which included a brief but acute bout of serious introspection and reevaluation, after which I deemed myself one fry short of a Happy Meal, clinically speaking. In other words, I went temporarily mad bonkers crazy. But today when I woke up I was back to my old self. I had my familiar bounce in my step, and I was even more buoyant and bubbly than before, like I'd been wearing my mom's ankle weights my whole life and just remembered to take them off. A whole section of my brain felt like it had been gutted and renovated and remodeled, unnecessary walls removed, ceiling raised, bathroom and kitchen appliances replaced, indoor/outdoor swimming pool and Jacuzzi added.

At first it seemed like a bad thing, a terrible thing, but turns out that going cuckoo for Coco Puffs is good for the soul, cleanses the senses and promotes growth. Now I spent my free time recalibrating my hopes and dreams while simultaneously disciplining my ego by upping my threshold for the psychological pain and suffering brought on by everyday life.

As I retrace the steps of my recent demise and rebirth, it appears that the Lemonade Project set off a disastrous domino effect of bad luck that bankrupted me emotionally, and in a reactionary state of mind I made a rash decision and directed my disappointment at the holiest of holies, my lord savior, creator and controller of the universe, the man, the myth, the legend: Abraham Lincoln the Penny. Ding-dong, the witch is dead, and so was my penny-worshiping cult! Just like that, Jim Jones! My ninety-eight-percent-zinc idolatry evaporated into thin air. It was time to stand on my own two feet, time to shed the shackles of superstition, the training wheels of spirituality, and take some responsibility for myself. I was ten and not getting any younger. I might have wanted to be agnostic, but that was merely wishful thinking, because I was clearly a classic closet monotheist mindlessly worshiping at the feet of Fortuna, and now I was finished. I squirted on a dollop of Purell and wiped my hands clean. For good.

I read a blog once that said Kung Fu legend Bruce Lee never got mad about anything, not even perturbed, not even if he stubbed his toe, which he did on several occasions. "I can't afford the luxury of anger," he once told a blogger. "Anger releases energy that is too precious to waste, particularly when I'm busy obliterating the deadliest street fighters in the world on a daily basis." Which is so true. I couldn't agree with him more about that, and if we were the same age and went to the same school and refuted the same religions and played tetherball at approximately the same level, we'd be best friends. I was sure of it.

The bell rang. It was Mr. Dobalina time.

14

"Evel Knievel was an American daredevil and holder of a Guinness World Record for breaking the most bones---four hundred and thirty-three---in one lifetime. He's famous for so many other things too, aside from his badass name, including his failed attempt to jump the Snake River on a steam-powered rocket cycle. At the height of Evel's success, what many consider the highest honor there is, at least for an American, was bestowed upon him: to have a roller coaster at Six Flags named after you. And this is what he had to say about it. 'I've been thrilling people all my life with death-defying stunts, and if I've proven only one thing, it's that after you take a spectacular fall, all you have to do is get right back up and try again. And then you're never a failure. And I can't think of a better way to convey that message than by partnering with Six Flags in Peoria, Illinois, for the debut of the downright stupidest, looptiest, kookiest, craziest roller coaster ever! And that's not even the best part. The best part is that we're expecting the line to ride the coaster to be the longest line in recorded history, anywhere in the world! Spanning all the way out of the amusement park, past the parking lot, around the corner, past the Howard Johnson's and up to Milwaukee and then over, some think, as far as Omaha, maybe, God willing, even Salt Lake City. Needless to say, I'm thrilled to be part of this; but if the coaster happens to crash, which it really shouldn't, remember, don't just lie there and die, first stop any immediate bleeding you might have, then assist women and children and the elderly, and then pull yourself up and out of the rubble, and get right back in line and do it all over again.'"

Mr. Dobalina paused for a sip of water, and Daffodil seized the opportunity to ask a question. "Evel Knievel sounds really cool, Mr. Dobalina. I like his flamboyant sense of style, but how does this relate to whatever it is you're teaching us?"

"That's an excellent question Daffodil. The truth is I'm not exactly sure. What I can tell you is this: Evel Knievel is an example of one of the most original thinkers of the modern era."

I nodded my head fervently as Mr. Dobalina continued to lecture, mainly because I usually agreed with anything that Mr. Dobalina had to say, and also because I was intrigued by this Evel Knievel character, and also because how dare Daffodil question Mr. Dobalina.

"Against all odds, Evel refused to be influenced by the media and general assumptions of what's acceptable, traditional, conventional, logical, practical, legitimate, or even intelligent. He was a scientist of self-destruction, a pioneer who paved the way for others. He was a revolutionary who made it cool to fail in spectacular fashion, particularly while live on TV, wearing a jumpsuit and a cape with tassels, no less, as millions of people watched in awe. Oh, and by the way, he was born right here in the fourth-largest but forty-fourth-least-populated and ethnically diverse state in the union, the land of the shining mountains, the last best place, our beloved Montana. I tell you this, students, because people like Evel Knievel make our state and our country and our whole world a better place, and he started out right here in our home state of Montana, just like you little twerps. Evel Knievel had a simple dream, kids: to jump his bicycle as far as possible. This could be any one of you. All you have to do is try and fail and try again and fail again and try and fail again and again and again, and break a few hundred bones while you're at it, and then you'll have succeeded."

Mr. Dobalina went on to rhapsodize about Abraham Lincoln, who had apparently failed to win dozens of elections on his path to becoming one of the great presidents and US currencies, the man responsible for drafting the Emancipation Proclamation.

As Mr. Dobalina went on, I couldn't help but feel like his words were intended solely for my benefit. Was it possible that he had heard through the grapevine about my unlucky loss on the tetherball court, or how I failed to sell one single glass of lemonade and nearly got arrested, or how I got bubble gum all over my favorite pants, completely ruining them, or how I hit my head, bumped my nose, and became an indentured servant? Maybe, I guess. The press is relentless, but under no condition could he possibly have known about the dramatic and unexpected retirement of my Abe Lincoln coin collection. Or was he an omniscient author who knows everything? Not at this point in the story. Maybe, or maybe not, Mr. Dobalina was having me trailed by a gumshoe or a shoofly or the FBI. Either way, I didn't care. He could do whatever he wanted, he had just inspired me more than ever before with his glamorous tales of heroic failure. I wanted to rush out into the world with reckless abandon and triumphantly fail, bigger and better than anyone ever had!

This was an epiphany for me, and although my track record with epiphanies wasn't perfect, it was the real deal, a eureka moment; like a prophecy without the middleman, it came directly from the source. The teakettle of my imagination whistled like a locomotive, bringing one extraordinary idea into ultra high-definition focus. And just like that my life had purpose, meaning, direction. I had a new dream to propel me forward. Something important, noble, a way to serve the boys and girls of Bumpkinville and Montana and the world, and to stop wasting time on bush league baloney. Drum roll, please. Say hello to your newest public servant, aka the future President of the entire Planet. It was my undeniable destiny to become a baby-kissin', handshakin' whistle-stopper. I'd probably become the greatest, most worshiped politician ever! If Abe could fail that many times and still win, and Evel could break that many bones and still walk, why couldn't I? By combining jaw-dropping daredevil stunt work with visionary policy making, flying dangerously close to socialism without ever entering her air space, and with plenty of public speaking supported by an array of guerrilla marketing tactics, I'd be sure to grab people's attention and win their votes. Simple as that. Then, as their leader and lawmaker, I'd make a difference, why not. And one day, if I did my job well, selflessly, virtuously, I might find my face on the side of a coin, maybe even a roller coaster.

The bell rang, interrupting my reverie. Daffodil cornered me in the hallway after class. "Mr. Dobalina's lecture was all over the place today," she said. "I mean, don't get me wrong, he's fascinating, but is he, you know, a little bit wacko?"

"Wacko!" I repeated, a tad insulted, "God, no." I laughed to myself. "He's only GQ's coolest guy in the universe runner-up. Two years in a row."

"Is that true?"

I nodded. "Can I talk to you about this?" I said, waving the to-do list in her face.

"Of course," she said, "thank you for being so responsive, that's an important part of the job. Never wait for me to come to you, always anticipate. Anticipation is the key. If you're anticipating my every desire every second of every day we shouldn't have any problems."

I was speechless for a second. Then I said, "For the record, my name is Willy Nilly. It's not William mother-loving Nilliam! How in the world you ever came up with that ridiculous name I will never know. Second, *our* business is *our* business, which means that it's nobody *else's* business, i.e., e.g., everyone in school doesn't need to know I'm your personal assistant. Capiche?" I took a breath and felt a tinge of satisfaction regarding my brevity and clarity with a dash of Italian flair, but Daffodil stonewalled me, no response at all. So I waited. We played chicken. Finally she flinched.

"Sure, I get it, I understand. Mum's the word." She pretended to zip her lips closed and throw away the key.

"If people were to find out that I worked for you---for a girl, a new girl, for free---it could be disastrous. Can you imagine? At the very least I look like a weakling, at best, a pushover. Not a lot of upside."

"I see your point, but do you happen to have a minute right now to go over the to-do list? I'm eager to get that clock ticking, since your thirty days of servitude don't officially start till we get started."

How annoying, I thought. "Let's meet out front after school," I said.

"Okay," she agreed. "That works for me."

I nodded in approval of her approval.

"And by the way," she said, "I thought you might like to know that I named my turtle after the greatest Kung Fu legend ever, the one and only---"

"Bruce Lee?"

"Yes! Bruce Lee!"

She seemed surprised. I was dumbfounded. Was this another of life's practical jokes? How could Daffodil possibly know that I worshiped at the altar of Bruce Lee? Was this life imitating art or art imitating life? I was so confused.

I chuckled ironically to myself. "You mean to tell me that you just coincidentally named Bruce Lee Bruce Lee?"

"How else would I have done it?"

"I don't know, but you couldn't have come up with a better name if I had done it. Bruce Lee is on my list of all-time favorite human beings!"

"How nice for you," she said.

"What are the chances we'd both love Bruce Lee?"

"It's coincidental. I'm curious, though, who else is on your list?"

"Oh, just a bunch of oddballs. Bruce Lee is by far the best. There's no question about that."

"Tell me the others."

"You won't know who they are."

"That's why I want you to tell me. So I know who Bruce Lee will be hanging out with in your imagination."

"Well, there's Sergey Bubka, the undisputed pole-vaulting world champion, twenty feet, one inch. He's held both the indoor and outdoor world records for twenty years and counting. And Cornelius Drebbel, who built the very first submersible submarine in 1620. Curt Jones, who's the inventor and former CEO of Dippin' Dots. Last I heard he had filed for Chapter 11 bankruptcy, and is in a major corporate restructuring period, but that doesn't negate the monumental achievement it was to flash-freeze ice cream mix in liquid nitrogen. I can't imagine the world without it."

Daffodil seemed taken aback. "Oh," was all she said.

I had her right where I wanted her, off balance and a little confused, so I seized the opportunity and went in for the kill. "As far as reading you to sleep at night and waking you up the next day reading the exact same book, it's just not gonna happen." I paused a few seconds to let that sink in. "For one thing, the commute would be a nightmare on my pogo stick. Imagine the blisters."

"I was just kidding about *Finnegans Wake*. It's nearly impossible to read that book under any circumstance. I just wanted to see how gullible you were. I was testing your gullibility level. It's pretty high, I'm afraid, but we can work on that."

"Okay, so you were also just kidding about bottling your teardrops, great. I was trying to imagine how in the world that was going to work."

Daffodil scrunched her face in the most peculiar way, as if both her chin and forehead simultaneously had unbearable itches that she wasn't allowed to scratch. After unscrunching her face she said, "Actually, I meant that part. To be honest, I've been crying a lot lately, an inordinate amount. I'm not sure if it's because of my grandpa or because I miss my friends back home, but I've been crying a lot more than usual and bottling my tears, which have always had a very distinct raspberry flavor to them. It's subtle but unmistakable. You'll love them. Everyone does."

"So are you serious right now, for instance? Because it sounds like you're kidding."

"No, I'm serious. All kidding aside, I've invented a teardrop catcher so I can bottle my tears, chill them, and save them for special occasions."

"I'm trying to take you seriously right now, but it's hard."

"I apologize. To make it easier, from now on assume that everything I say is serious, and if I happen to crack a joke, I'll preface it with 'this is a joke.'"

"That'll kill your timing."

"Which do you prefer, confusion or comedy?"

"I'd rather laugh and be confused."

"Then it's settled. We'll meet after school and I'll start teaching you how to be my assistant."

"And I'll start teaching Bruce Lee how to do karate," I joked.

"I'd be very surprised if you could teach him karate," she said.

"I'm not suggesting he can *be* Bruce Lee, or even a Teenage Mutant Ninja Turtle, but why not a yellow belt or an orange one? It's not out of the question."

"I highly doubt that a turtle, even my turtle, who is a brilliant and talented turtle, can learn karate, and he certainly won't be wearing any belts."

"It's a metaphorical belt," I said, shaking my head. "And if you think it's so impossible then perhaps you'd like to put a little wager on it?"

"You're crazy, because this is a terrible bet for you, Willy. Trust me."

"You're scared."

"And you have a gambling problem."

"Don't patronize me. Let's bet."

"Is the bet whether or not you can teach Bruce Lee karate?"

"Yep."

"How long will it take you?"

"Maybe a year, could be less."

"And what's the bet for?"

I went for broke, because I had nothing to lose. "Joint custody of Bruce Lee."

"No way."

"Hear me out. If I manage to pull a miracle out of my ass, then it's only fair that you agree to split him with me---not in half, that's disgusting, but his time. And if I don't succeed, like you're so sure I won't, then I'll be your personal assistant for the rest of my life or one full year, whichever comes first. I'll be at your beck and call, and I won't quit or file an underage employment grievance with the state under any condition."

Daffodil stuck out her hand with oomph, eager to shake and make it official.

"Wait," I said, feeling a twinge of self-doubt because of her unwavering self-confidence. "I need a second to think about this." I considered all the unlikely stories involving animals I had seen on TV, like Jim the chimpanzee from Waikiki who learned how to surf the Pipeline in under a year, or the dolphin at SeaWorld in Orlando who could hula-hoop while levitating above the water posing for photos, or the elephant from Kathmandu who could tap-dance and play the sax better than Kenny G, all of which made me believe that it was possible for a turtle to learn some basic karate moves. Crazier things had happened, and with a name like Bruce Lee, what choice did he have? It was his fate, not mine. I had to try for his sake, he was entitled to that, it was his birthright, his karma and destiny, and who was I to stand in the way? That I had absolutely zero karate training didn't concern me. I had seen most of Jackie Chan's ouevre and a few of John Woo's later films when I was younger. And there were always YouTube videos to help demonstrate complicated maneuvers. Bottom line, I was never going to find a better excuse than this to make the time to learn karate, so I threw caution to the wind.

"It's a bet," I said, extending my hand.

We shook like we were heads of state from two notoriously unfriendly countries and this was a long-overdue diplomatic relations photo op promoting goodwill and civility. Together we faked smiles as an imaginary newspaper photographer snapped a photo with a flash-lamp (filled with magnesium powder and potassium chlorate) that exploded all over us, but not before capturing the historical significance of this landmark moment on celluloid forever.

15

Not that it's a big deal or anything, and I don't like to brag, but I probably should have mentioned this sooner: I can yo-yo like nobody's business. It's one of my best qualities. Is yo-yoing a quality, or is it a talent? It doesn't matter, because I'm a yo-yo artist in my mind, and of the highest caliber, like da Vinci or Basquiat or Banksy. To be honest, I'm not entirely self-taught, I did attend a yo-yo sleep-away summer camp three years ago to hone my skills and make some new friends, but by my own estimation I was already one of the best yo-yoers in the country for my age. For instance, if yo-yoing was a school sport, I would be a living legend in Bumpkinville, varsity captain, first-string all-American, dating a cheerleader and cutting classes, but it's not and presumably never will be. I can walk the dog and shoot the moon. I have a signature move, my trademark, figuratively speaking---I haven't actually trademarked it, but I should, because it's the move that put me on the map, an undeniable crowd pleaser called the William Saroyan, aka the Daring Young Man on the Flying Trapeze.

Daffodil arrived as I was attempting another difficult and impressive maneuver called the Bank Deposit, which is an ideal trick to finish a set with, but it's very hard to get just right, and dangerous when you don't. Most yo-yo artists practice for a lifetime before attempting this in the presence of a girl. But not me, I was a daredevil. I had the experience, the desire, the focus, and if I succeeded Daffodil would be right where I wanted her, eating out of the palm of my hand.

This is how the Bank Deposit works: step 1, pull your left pocket away from your pants as far as possible; step 2, throw a hard sleeper between your legs---and be careful; step 3, let the yo-yo swing around your leg and into your left pocket; step 4, voilà, presto, finito, you're a genius, the people love you, hurray hurray; step 5, take a bow. Regrettably, I got caught up on step 2 (the between-the-legs part).

Daffodil snickered a little, at least I thought she did, but I couldn't be sure, so I shot her the evil eye just in case. We walked in silence to her house until I took pity on her and decided to share my exciting news, my desire to become an iconoclastic daredevil politician.

"You mean a heathen?"

"What? No, of course not, more like a maverick or a nonconformist or

Batman, not a heathen."

Despite her childish taunting, Daffodil surprisingly seemed to like the idea, but she was curious to know what exactly I meant by daredevil, more specifically what I was planning to do that was daring or devilish. It was a good question, I was curious myself. And for some unexplainable reason she also wanted to know what my politics were. "Are you a Democrat or a Republican, Libertarian or Green?" she asked. "Or maybe you're a member of a minor party like the Tea Party or the Pirate Party, which is a pro-internet party in case you don't know."

"I'm currently unaffiliated," I said, "but leaning toward throwing my own party."

Daffodil revealed that she was a member of the Green Party, and proceeded to list the party's twelve guiding principles: grassroots democracy, social justice, equal opportunity, ecological wisdom, nonviolence, decentralization, community-based economics, gender equality, respect for diversity, personal and global responsibility, and future sustainability. She went on to stress the fact that the Green Party does not accept contributions, donations, or even suggestions of any kind from corporations or convicted felons, particularly both, unless they were wrongly convicted, either for a crime they didn't commit, or for a crime they committed that shouldn't have been a crime in the first place, e.g., carrying an ice cream cone in your back pocket, wearing a fake mustache to church, or flicking boogers in the wind.

Eventually, after meandering down a barren road for what felt like forever, we arrived at the pearly gates of Daffodil's palace---or was it a castle? I can never remember the difference. Towering overhead, nearly touching the clouds, was the most extraordinary piece of surreal architecture I'd ever seen, especially for Bumpkinville, not that I'd seen everything the town had to offer, but this was something else. Imagine the Neuschwanstein Castle in Germany, the one from *Sleeping Beauty*, made entirely from wood---teak, I think. Was it the first entirely wooden castle in the world with a rustic western ranch motif? Probably. A lot of splinters were suffered building that, I thought, a carpenter's ultimate nightmare and greatest achievement. Instead of farm animals everywhere there were peacocks. And above the driveway, before you crossed the log drawbridge over the moat, there was a flashing hot-pink neon sign: Peggy's Peacock Palace. This immediately reminded me of Ruth's Chris Steakhouse, which has always been a source of great irritation because I just don't understand that possessive before Chris, which seems to indicate that Ruth is the owner of Chris and Chris is the owner of the steakhouse, which would make Chris Ruth's slave, which is illegal, or maybe Ruth is Chris's mom, but either way it's got to be a stifling relationship. I thought about writing them a letter.

I quelled my consternation long enough to ask, "Who's Peggy?"

"She's my grandmother," Daffodil said. "The property was originally a peacock breeding ranch. It's not anymore, but we still have a few, and we can't stop them from having their fun once in a while."

"That's a relief. I was afraid we had another Ruth's Chris Steakhouse on our hands."

"I know exactly what you mean," Daffodil said. "Let's go in, shall we?"

We crossed the moat and entered what I can honestly say is, was, and will always be the most spectacularly unexpected wonderland I've ever seen. Surrounding the wooden castle was a sprawling mega-sports complex unmatched by any in the world. There was every imaginable field, court, rink, range, cage, lane, wall, and pool.

I had either been struck by lightning like my old man, and was now standing at the gates of heaven next to a little angel---or devil---named Daffodil, or I was alive and well and the world was more phantasmagorical than I had previously realized.

"Wow," was all I could say. There was a maddening profusion of topiary in all the usual shapes and sizes, mainly animals and vegetables and geometric shapes, along with the occasional common household object, like a dustpan or a couch or a blender. There was a raging river that snaked its way through the property, and a three-hole golf course tangled around it, with an archery range, a fifteen-foot-tall wooden Jenga (with an electric scaffolding machine, a ladder, and a pair of stilts for better positioning) across from a basketball court, a tennis court, a volleyball court---or was it a badminton court, I couldn't tell---a roller derby rink, and would you believe it, none other than a top-of-the-line, state-of-the-art tetherball court---three of them, to be exact.

I could have stood there forever staring at all the theoretical fun I could have, until it dawned on me that Daffodil might not only be a world-class tetherball dynamo, she might also be one of the world's greatest multi-sport athletes ever. My god. How did she even find time to go to school with all these games to be played? No wonder she needed an assistant.

We stepped onto a moving walkway, aka a horizontalator, that was camouflaged into the environment with patches of grass and plants and flowers, and were whisked away to Daffodil's personal wing of the palace. Inside was a fish tank surpassed in quality and size by only five others in the world: the Pacific, the Atlantic, the Indian, the Arctic, and the Southern. (In the spring of 2000, after countless defamation suits---and who can blame them?---the International Hydrographic Organization finally acknowledged the Southern as an Ocean, even threw in a compliment or two.)

Bruce Lee was living the life of Riley in the world's most luxurious turtle tank---Robin Leach would have been proud. His pad made Sea World look like Sesame Street. The tank was made entirely from glass and steel and meticulously crafted, hand-carved mahogany, and it wasn't just another pretty face either, it had personality. It was filled with exotic and endangered fish and plants from all over the world, not to mention Bruce Lee; there were even a few miniature sunken pirate ships for decoration, with real gold and jewels inside. Shamu the killer whale would have died and gone to heaven for the chance to live or even vacation here, and so would Flipper and Free Willy (no relation to me). Give me a snorkel and pair of floaties and I'd live in that tank too.

The moment I saw Bruce Lee, the same unexplainable feeling I had in the pet store returned with a vengeance. Powerful radio waves seemed to emanate from him, as if there was a car stereo in my brain and I was scanning from one static station to another, searching for a signal from WTRTL.

Bruce Lee paddled over to an anatomically correct rock, climbed onto it, kicked one leg over the other, and started nibbling on a chocolate-dipped grasshopper. When he finally noticed that I was watching him, his neck slowly extended and his big inquisitive eyeballs zeroed in on me. Then the gravelly baritone voice of someone who sounded a lot like Stacy Keach began to reverberate inside my brain. Bingo, I had cracked the turtle's radio station. I was inside his shell. Or was he inside my skull?

"Yes," he said, or someone said, but if not him, then who?

I turned and smiled at Daffodil sheepishly, the same way Brad Pitt might smile at Angelina Jolie if he silently farted and was hoping she hadn't smelled it. Apparently Daffodil hadn't smelled it, or heard it, in this case.

"Yes, Willy, I'm talking to you."

Wow, this is weird, I thought.

"No, it's not that weird, not really, not if you compare it to some of the early illustrations of Edward Gorey, like in *The Doubtful Guest* or *The Glorious Nosebleed* or especially the *The Epiplectic Bicycle*. That is hardly the point, though, my young friend, your being able to speak telepathically is all that matters. Congratulations, it's very uncommon for land mammals, you should be proud. For dolphins and whales it's a piece of cake, but it's much easier in the water. In any case, this works out well for us. We can keep each other company. It can get awfully lonely in here sometimes without anyone to talk to, as nice as this place is," Bruce Lee thought to me.

"But what about Daffodil? She must be fluent in telepathy if I am."

"Nope, not even conversational. It's too bad, and a little surprising for a girl from such a cosmopolitan family, but if you don't learn to not speak when you're young enough to grasp the simplicity of it, you'll never learn."

"But I never learned," I thought.

"Your father taught you as a baby, which is the best time to learn. Around two years old is ideal."

"Interesting," I thought. "But I have absolutely no recollection of that at all."

"Yet you can hear me loud and clear, and I'm inside this glass tank underwater, and I haven't moved my lips."

There was no denying any of that.

"Let me ask you a question. Is there anything else you can remember not learning when you were a baby?" Bruce thought.

I felt like I was losing my mind, my identity, my individuality, and about to wake up from a really good dream right before the best part.

"You're wide awake, Willy, and Daffodil doesn't know we're telepathically communicating, she just thinks you're stranger than she thought you were, and she already thought you were really strange to begin with."

"But I don't understand. How could my dad have known telepathy without my mom or my uncle finding out about it?"

"Your father learned telepathy from his father, who learned it from his father, who learned it from his father, who was one of the co-founders of the Turkish branch of the Telepathic Society. Nowadays telepathy has fallen so far out of fashion because there are so few people who know how to speak it. After your father's death you never thought about it again, not even to yourself, but it's like riding a bike, as they say: once you know, you never forget."

Sheepishly I turned my head toward Daffodil. She was staring at me peculiarly, probably the same way I had been staring at Bruce Lee. Trying to reclaim some semblance of normality, I abruptly inquired about her tear catcher.

"I thought you'd never ask," she said. "Follow me."

I thought a quick goodbye to Bruce Lee as she led me down a long dark hallway lit by candles and lined with a series of oil portraits in ornate gold frames, featuring family members and friends with either their ears or their noses missing. How strange. She led me to her bedroom, which was better than your average, you could say, with a unicorn merry-go-round and hundreds of toys and clothes and contraptions and gizmos scattered about on a couple of acres of pink shag carpet.

"Here it is," she said, pulling a black satin cloth from a jewelry display pedestal to reveal what looked like an eyelash curler glued to a glass bottle.

"Fascinating," I said, scrutinizing it.

"It works," Daffodil said. "I filled a few bottles last night. Would you like a glass?"

I nodded emphatically. I was thirsty. Daffodil rang a little bell, and a servant appeared moments later, impeccably dressed in an Armani tuxedo, ruffled shirt, bow tie, and black bowler. He was carrying a silver salver holding two chilled champagne glasses and white satin napkins with the Peacock family insignia embroidered elegantly in the corners.

We clinked our glasses. "To the octopus," I said, "the true unsung hero of our time."

Daffodil paused. "What in the world are you talking about?"

"I'm talking about the octopus as archetype. These eight-armed, translucent, suction-cupped, highly intelligent, and highly emotional creatures make the ultimate sacrifice. They trade their own lives for the chance to have children, and what could be nobler than that? The male octopus dies almost immediately after mating, and the female dies of starvation shortly after her eggs have hatched. Plus, octopuses have three hearts. Did you know that? Three! Which makes me think they might experience emotions exponentially, to the third heart power. There was even an octopus named Paul, born in Britain but living in Germany, who could predict the future, but only for European soccer matches, which coincidentally was all anyone cared about. Paul correctly predicted the outcome of all seven matches in the 2010 FIFA World Cup, including the finals! Obviously, with a talent like that, he was a national hero, god rest his soul."

Daffodil raised her glass. "You had me at three hearts," she said. "To Paul the Octopus."

We clinked again, exchanging capricious looks, and then I tipped Daffodil's teardrops into my mouth. Eureka! As promised, they were raspberry-flavored. I licked my lips. "Your depression tastes delicious," I said.

Daffodil smiled.

"But be honest, did you add flavoring or a sweetener? Because it's got the perfect balance, delicate but intense, and not too sweet. I won't tell anyone if you did, I promise."

"No, I didn't add anything. It's all natural, one hundred percent organic, no preservatives, and it's even kosher, because my butler is also a rabbi. And a registered notary public too, just in case."

I held the glass to my nose and smelled the sweet aroma. I took another sip and swirled it in my mouth, carefully considering all the pleasant sensations it provoked. It was spicy and supple and round and effervescent all at once, it had achieved harmonious fusion. And like dry ice on a hot day, it immediately evaporated from your taste buds, leaving you desperate for more. The complexity and character of these tears were off the charts. I hadn't come across a more expressive beverage in years, if ever.

"This is better than Vitamin Water or Snapple or Capri Suns," I boldly declared. I wondered if my own tears were fruit-flavored. Was this a more common phenomenon than I'd realized? "Do you eat an inordinate amount of raspberries?"

"Depends on what you consider inordinate, I guess."

"More than five a day, I'd say, or thirty-five a week."

"If that includes raspberry frozen yogurt, raspberry jelly, raspberry toothpaste, and raspberry face cream, then yes, I eat a lot of raspberries."

"I bet we could sell your raspberry teardrops and make a lot of money," I said. "We could market them like champagne for rich kids."

"You think so?"

"Yeah, if we had a cool bottle design, a snazzy logo, a celebrity endorsement, and an advertising budget, I think we could sell millions of bottles. I'm just spitballing here, but a fifth of Dom Perignon might retail for a hundred and fifty bucks or more, which means it wholesales for around a hundred, so if we assume we can sell five million bottles at a hundred bucks a bottle, we'd gross five hundred million a year for starters."

"Fabulous," Daffodil said. "Just one problem."

"Which is?"

"Five million bottles of tears a year is about fourteen thousand bottles a day, which means I would die of dehydration and depression. I don't think my tear ducts could handle that kind of volume. And besides, you wouldn't know what to do with five hundred million dollars anyway."

"Oh yes I would," I said without a heartbeat of hesitation. "I'd run for mayor on a platform of allowing the unrestricted free trade and distribution of lemonade, or any beverage, anywhere within town limits, no permits required, no questions asked.

"That's the stupidest idea I've ever heard."

This didn't faze me. Clearly she was not a qualified political analyst, as many people aren't. No need to take it personally. This was a new idea for me as well.

"Now that I think about it," I said, "there's so much money in the teardrop business that if you and I were to split the take, could be a hundred million each after taxes, and with that kind of cash, not only could I be mayor, I could run for president of the United States and win, because that's how it works."

"But you're only eleven, so there's that."

"Ten, actually," I admitted for no good reason.

"My god," she said as considerately as you can.

"Enough about me. What would you do with a hundred million?"

"I'd hire Frank Gehry, or Howard Roark maybe, if he was alive, to design and build thousands of low-cost, high-style, ultra-modern communal apartment buildings for homeless people to live in, all over the world."

"But how do you verify that someone is actually homeless and not just pretending to be so they can live there for free?"

"If whoever you're referring to prefers to live in a no-income communal apartment building with other formerly homeless residents, then they're wholeheartedly welcome, even if their parents live in a castle like me."

"Okay, so maybe your idea is more altruistic than mine," I conceded, "but mine tastes better and is more refreshing. And I'm not suggesting this, but if we were to collaborate, it looks like we'd have all the bases covered. Just saying."

The thought of homeless people, or the idea of collaborating with me, perhaps, or an unrelated wave of sadness swept over Daffodil. She sniffled. Our eyes locked for a second. We shared a moment. I reached for the tear catcher.

16

Uncle Tunafish picked me up at Daffodil's castle a few hours later than promised. I was sitting on the curb by the drawbridge, on the street side of the moat, staring at the moon, punch-drunk on teardrops, when his bug finally sputtered up.

"Nice place," he said as I got in and buckled my seat belt.

"Yeah, not too shabby," I said, "but what do you know about telepathy?"

"Why do you ask?"

"No particular reason." I looked away and whistled wistfully to myself until I ran out of breath. "My friend Daffodil has a turtle named Bruce Lee that I'm pretty sure was talking to me without actually talking to me," I said finally. "Do you know what I mean?"

"Sure, you probably ate too much candy," Uncle Tunafish said. "Try sleeping it off. If you're still hearing voices in the morning, then you might have a bad case of schizophrenia, which is basically incurable and could lead to electric shock therapy or worse, but otherwise you'll be fine."

I settled into the passenger seat to ponder the nature of politics and the passing scenery: trees and fields and fences and barns and birds and horses and cows and telephone poles and the occasional house and truck. Politics meant power and control, but that alone was boring, and not worth the effort, it needed something else. Danger?

Political daredevil had a nice ring to it. Very nice. So nice, in fact, that I could intuitively tell it could very well become my future occupation, my lifelong obsession and calling and hobby all wrapped into one. But before I got carried away, I had to develop some sound political strategies and guiding philosophical principles for my new political party, which needed a snazzy name, something evocative and memorable, playful and serious, like the Inside Out Party or the Upside Down Party or the Pajama Party. I wanted to be mayor of Bumpkinville, as a springboard to becoming president of the United States, at which point I would restore and quadruple NASA's budget for space exploration---what could be more important planet-wise?---and cut the military budget to zero, using the massive savings to fund education reform, because you don't have to be a rocket scientist to understand that if every country keeps upping their military budget and lowering their education budget, there will come a day when everyone has too many weapons and too little intelligence to keep from blowing themselves up.

Was it too ambitious to start with a mayoral campaign? Perhaps I could run for student council next year, when I was in seventh grade, but why go to all that trouble, and for what? I didn't see the point, and I didn't have that kind of time to mess around in the minor leagues. It was almost springtime and I was no chicken, which meant summer vacation was just around the corner, which meant that student council elections weren't for another six months or more, which was roughly a million mayfly lifetimes away. Not to mention the power and prestige of the mayor's office compared to the student council. It just didn't have the pizzazz I was looking for. I asked myself what Shaun White, the ginger-head snowboard god of gods, would do in my situation, and then it was obvious: he would go big or go home. It was time to drop into the political half pipe and do some tricks. So mayor it was, for all the obvious reasons, power and money and respect, and while I was at it, I might as well do some good too. I wanted to be mayor and I wanted it now. I needed to leverage my youth while I still had it.

The following days and nights flew by. I was a man possessed. When I wasn't assisting Daffodil I lived in the library, researching famous politicians, military leaders, stuntmen, martial arts experts, rock stars, comedians, and cartoonists. What I discovered was that rock stars and military leaders had very little in common except for enormous egos and a craving for somewhat perverse but stylish military uniforms. Martial arts experts and stuntmen and comedians and cartoonists, on the other hand, had a lot in common; they were all fiercely independent, idealistic, noble, hardworking, risk-taking, and self-deprecating, but not excessively. In short, they were everything I was, or hoped I would become if I wasn't already. Politicians, famous or not, weren't quite as interesting on the whole, aside from Lincoln; they were too compromising and middle-of-the road for my tastes; I would need to spice things up a little, break the mold, get crazy.

I read Bruce Lee's (not the turtle's) seminal work *Chinese Gung-Fu: The Philosophical Art of Self Defense*. I appreciated the irony of learning karate from Bruce Lee while simultaneously teaching it to Bruce Lee. There was one move in particular that I thought he would be capable of mastering. It was called the one-inch punch, the description of which is as follows: stand upright, knees slightly bent, right foot forward, right arm bent but extended, shoulder back, right fist approximately one inch away from your sparring partner's (or enemy's) chest. Without retracting your arm at all, forcibly deliver a devastating punch while largely maintaining your upright posture and sending your partner hurtling backwards into a wall, or through a wall, as the case may be.

I had many telepathic conversations with Bruce Lee during this time. He explained the general nature of consciousness to me, how we observe the world through our eyes and ears and nose and fingers and toes but what we sense is converted and structured in our mind through the language of words, and then words are turned into labels and labels into ideas and ideas into reality. He explained that the world as we perceive it is merely a reflection of the inside of our brains, which is merely a reflection of the entire unknown universe.

This led to long debates over the merits of structuralism versus existentialism, and an Aristotelian proof of the proposition that modern cooking shows are eerily similar to ancient forms of alchemical practice. "Alchemy," Bruce explained, "is the inexplicable transmutation of something common into something magical, with the ultimate goal of discovering a universal cure for all diseases and prolonging life indefinitely. At the heart of alchemy is a spiritual process of inner transformation, metaphorically represented by the transmutation of lead into gold. Think of an alchemist as a cowboy in a spaghetti western on a quest for the regeneration of the human soul, not for money."

Which I agreed with, mostly. Well, not exactly. I wanted the money too, but only to help facilitate my inner transformation, of course.

"It will come," he assured me, "be patient, you're only ten," and then he revealed to me that he was in fact an alchemist himself, and a certified shaman's assistant, and in all modesty a fairly decent watercolorist to boot.

As the school year dwindled to an end, I found myself spending all my free time with Bruce Lee and Daffodil. These were our salad days (as Douglas Fairbanks Jr. might have said, or H. I. McDunnough), the days when we were young and naive, fresh as a Wendy's salad bar on weekend afternoons, green in judgment and cold in blood.

I don't want to blame Bruce Lee entirely, but it seemed to me that my other two friends were no longer my friends because of the green-eyed monster. They didn't come right out and say it, but I could tell, anyone could tell, it was obvious. They were jealous, who wouldn't be? It was also possible that my recently recovered telepathic powers had made me overly sensitive as of late, but I certainly wasn't imagining the continuous brush-off I got on the playground from Tilo and Mosquito. In that sense, I guess, everyone's telepathic to some degree. In their defense, it's possible that their blatant neglect of me was an overreaction to my unintentional prior neglect of them and that we were embroiled in the quintessential cyclical modern relationship quagmire that befuddles us all.

I was an exemplary executive assistant. I think Daffodil would agree. I fulfilled and effectuated her every request, and spritzing her face, which was embarrassing at first, became one my favorite tasks. In the blink of an eye my month of servitude flew by, and next thing I knew Daffodil and her dad were departing by seaplane for Turks and Caicos, deep in the West Indies. Daffodil was officially the luckiest girl in the world, as far as I could tell. She had been accepted into an ultra-exclusive spring-break sleep-away pirate camp that featured, among other mind-blowing activities, scuba diving for sunken treasure, learning authentic pirate dialect, sword fighting with a peg leg and a hook for a hand, and the camp's signature offering, walking the plank with style and grace to achieve the perfect plummet to your death.

A number of years ago, before his freezing and thawing, Daffodil's grandfather won a cutthroat bidding war on eBay (using a special bidding bot) for an authentic eighteenth-century treasure map, reportedly inscribed by the notorious seaside pirate/entrepreneur, Captain Blackbeard himself.

As the story goes, on what would become Blackbeard's final sail through the Caribbean, with his entire life's loot on board, things took an unexpected turn for the worse, forcing Blackbeard to ditch his treasure in a secret spot and draw a map so he could come back when it was more convenient, without assailants and tropical storms on his back. That was the treasure map Grandpa Peacock bought for sweet little Daffodil, and she was taking it with her so she'd have something to do in her spare time.

Pirateologists have estimated the potential value of the treasure to be as high as $1.2 billion and as low as a couple of crabs and some skeletons.

17

Over spring break, while Daffodil was underwater spelunking, Bruce Lee got to slum it at my place. He slept in the bathtub, so I got him a rubber duck and some sea-breeze-scented, nontoxic, organic bubbles to jazz things up. It was the least I could do for my soul mate, considering the deluxe aquarium he was accustomed to.

In the mornings, after discussing the symbolic meaning of our dreams and eating a light healthy breakfast, we hiked to the Penny Graveyard, where we limbered our muscles and quieted our minds with a gentle thirty-minute Ashtanga yoga practice, usually followed by a ferocious Kung Fu fight routine. Bruce Lee was a natural, no surprise. In the afternoons we studied the philosophies of the great masters. Bruce telepathically impersonated, with accents and mannerisms, everyone from Socrates and Jung to Theodor Geisel and Raymond Chandler and Kurt Vonnegut, and occasionally, time permitting, Steven Wright.

Kurt Vonnegut, via Bruce Lee, explained that a humanist is someone who decides to behave decently, with civility and kindness to others, without expectation of reward or punishment after death.

Raymond Chandler pointed out that a good detective never gets married and that there are a million and one different types of blondes out there, so don't lump them all together.

Theodor Geisel discussed the value of nonsense, already my forte. "I like nonsense," he said, "it wakes up the brain cells."

Carl Jung rhapsodized about his collective unconscious mind theory and how all humans share the same basic ancestral memories and experiences that unite us all. Like the Internet.

Socrates, our great-grandfather of reasoning, managed to reduce all knowledge and wisdom to the bare naked essentials, simplifying life into what is now considered the cornerstone of Western philosophy: "I know that I know nothing." It's important to point out that Socrates is specifically saying that he knows something.

And then there was Steven Wright, who famously discovered that the shin bone "is a device for finding furniture in the dark."

In the evenings Bruce usually relaxed from his exhausting philosophical performances by painting with watercolors while I read or wrote Mad Lib political speeches.

One afternoon I was suddenly interrupted by a tsunami of telepathic vibrations. I was minding my own business when Bruce Lee blurted out silently that I was ready to advance to the next level of Super Mario Bros. in the Nintendo of my life.

"Huh?" I said, putting down my autographed copy of *Don Quixote*, with original illustrations by Salvador Dali, which I found, surprisingly, in the Bumpkinville library.

Bruce smirked at me like the Cheshire cat, then wasted no time dictating a ludicrous list of items he needed from the store: the grocery store, the hardware store, the thrift store, the pet store, the department store, the candy store, the Apple store, the health food store, the shoe store, the discount store, the general store, and the convenience store. He said that he needed all these things to prepare an elixir and perform a superduper hocus-pocus conjuring act.

"What for?" I asked, and he said I'd see soon enough.

It took a few days to acquire everything on the list. A poster of David Hasselhoff in the nude but discreetly covered with shar-pei puppies, ten meters of double barbed wire stained with dried antelope blood, and seven stale green Gummy Bears were all easy to find. Three ripe kumquats and a partridge in a pear tree were more difficult. I ordered most of the items online from Amazon Prime (I'm finally a member), paying for them with the food and entertainment per diem that Daffodil had graciously left behind.

Our timing was impeccable, as it turned out. On the night of Bruce's big ceremony, a lunar eclipse was scheduled to coincide with launching me through the proverbial portal-pipe of life, which I innocently assumed would take me to the The Legend of Zelda.

Bruce prepared a bubbling caldron of magic potion that looked a lot like the vegetarian elk chili my mom sometimes made. I prepared some Lunchables and Capri Suns for later. I hadn't eaten all day, because a short fast before a spiritual ceremony can intensify the experience, so I was famished, both for food and for my metamorphosis. I was ready for anything, bring it on, just like the blown-away guy from the Maxell tape ads. I taunted destiny. I welcomed danger. I worshiped loud music. Turn me into a grotesque bug or a chair, I don't care, just do it already.

Bruce stirred the caldron as it cooked over a triangular fire pit that I had proudly helped design and build. I'd selected the location so it would be directly over the grave of my deceased penny collection, for closure. Trillions of stars sparkled daintily in the velvety blue-black night sky, which was alive and pulsating like the beating heart of a baby panda. The moon and the earth and the sun would soon be in perfect single-file alignment. Anal-retentive drill sergeants and dominatrices everywhere would be drooling with envy and delirious with pride at the sight of this temporary cosmic submission to linear order.

As the exact moment of alignment quickly approached, the chorus to "Total Eclipse of the Heart" got stuck on a permanent loop in my brain. Being a Bonnie Tyler fan, Bruce Lee knew the lyrics and started singing along. We belted it out telepathically, in a madcap Bizarro World duet. *Faster Than the Speed of Night* earned Bonnie the distinction of being the first and only Welsh singer to reach the number one spot on Billboard's Top 100 Chart, and now I knew why.

The moon slipped gracefully into its lunar-eclipse parking spot, parallel with the earth and the sun, a celestial country line dance on the intergalactic stage of eternity. Then the moon turned bright red, like a British tourist under a Jamaican sun. It was breathtaking. Words were ill equipped to describe this planetary poetry. And then, when we least expected it, a bolt of lightning zigzagged out of the sky, directly into Bruce Lee, who was standing right next to me, and blew him twenty feet in the air. He landed in a bush, upside down and enveloped in smoke. He was dead, it was obvious. I crawled toward him on my hands and knees, tears beginning to stream down my cheeks. The biggest relief of my life washed over me when I heard Bruce think, "Not exactly the way I planned that to work, but ta-da, we did it!"

"Thank god, you're alive," I said, retrieving him from the bush.

"We did it, Willy! We did it!"

Jumping up and down exuberantly, I asked, "What did we do?"

"We conjured the spirit gods."

"We did?"

"Yes!"

"And what did they say?"

"That was it."

"What was it?"

"That."

"Which was what?"

"What you just saw."

"I should have mentioned this sooner, I guess, but all my life I've suffered from a mild case of astraphobia, which drastically affects your reasoning skills when lightning strikes."

"You're not alone," Bruce said. "According to a 2007 survey, astraphobia is the third most prevalent phobia in the U.S., behind arachnophobia and social phobia."

"I didn't realize there was such a thing as a social phobia."

"Most cases go undiagnosed."

"I'm not surprised. But what did we succeed at, Bruce? What happened? I'm so confused."

"Now I turn into a holographic video projector and play you the message."

"Like R2-D2?"

"Similar, but in this case it's real. No puppets or computer-generated images."

"Is the message from Princess Leia?"

"No, smarty-pants, your father."

"You mean Darth Vader?"

"Don't be ridiculous. Are you ready?"

Bruce was not your typical turtle, there was no question about that, but raising the dead? Really? And on the exact spot where I'd buried all the pennies I'd been collecting on my Newton-inspired but stunningly original theory that they would bring me good luck proportionate to or greater than my dad's bad luck? But what could my dad possibly have to say to me? I looked at Bruce, who was zapping me with an intense gaze of grieve gravity.

"Trust me," he thought.

"Okay, I trust you. Let's do this."

"Good. Now flip me onto my back and spin me around as fast as you can."

"Like a dreidel?"

"Yeah, or a nondenominational spinning top. Let her rip, as fast as you can. It helps with the resolution."

Apparently this was no time for a game of patty-cake, so I grabbed Bruce and turned him over and spun him around like I was a Harlem Globetrotter and he was a basketball. It was tricky at first, gyroscopically balancing a turtle on the tip of my finger, but I got the hang of it pretty fast.

Once I reached what felt like an adequate rotation velocity, I lowered him to the ground, where he continued to spin like a whirling dervish at a discotheque in Constantinople on a Saturday night in the thirteenth century. Like the headlights on a Mack Truck, Bruce Lee's eyeballs began shining, and then I beheld a high-definition holographic apparition of my father, fifteen feet high, with what seemed to be THX Dolby Digital Surround Sound coming from his mouth. Watching your soul mate transform into a magical 3-D movie projector is weird, it truly is, so I did the only thing that made any sense at this point. I sat back to enjoy the show.

"I'm sorry I died, son," my dad began, which I appreciated, because to be honest, it was rude of him to die at such an inopportune time, when I was in my tenderest years. His handlebar mustache was neatly trimmed and waxed, his hair slicked back. He looked a lot less like a cowboy than I had imagined, more like an industrialist. His voice was vaguely familiar, but not familial. As he spoke, he flung his arms back and forth like a hysterical composer emphasizing a phrase.

"I've had a lot of time to think about my life, son, especially about you and your mom and Tunafish, and a lot of time to get my priorities straight. Which I have finally managed to do, believe it or not, although you could say I'm a day late and a dollar short, but you could also say better late than never. So here it is. In the moment I was electrocuted, three profound things occurred to me. Number one, that I had wasted my entire life trying to impress my father and fulfill his unrealized dreams instead of my own, which made me a total failure. Number two, that I wasn't necessarily a total failure because I still had you, Willy. And number three, which is related to number one and number two, was that if I hadn't spent my time hawking Frisbees and boomerangs to make my dad proud of me, I could have been riding waterslides all day. That's right, waterslides, I'm not embarrassed to say it, and not just riding them, designing them and building them too. As you know, this dream of mine was never realized, in large part because I didn't actually know about it when I was still alive. It took dying, funnily enough, to figure it out. But the point, Willy, is that my destiny is incomplete, my true love unfulfilled, our family legacy in jeopardy. However, Willy my boy, all is not lost. It's up to you to restore honor and dignity to me and the Nilly family name. In fact, it's your karmic responsibility. Look at it as the inheritance you never got. And it's so much better than money, right? Ideas like this are priceless. Now you have something meaningful to spend the rest of your life pursuing, which is the secret to happiness. Finding something you love, or at least that your father loved, and doing it every day. And ultimately, as long as you have a child of your own before you kick the bucket, a child who will selflessly dedicate their entire life to pursing your dream---which is really my dream---then you can't fail. Think of it as an endless relay race. All you have to do is pass the baton."

"Now wait a second," I interjected, my brain about to overheat. I had forgotten this wasn't a live video chat as opposed to a supernatural holographic dad-back-from-the-dead chat.

"I'm sure you have a million questions, Willy," my dad continued. "I certainly would, like why I taught you telepathy when you were two and a half and how it's been a Nilly family tradition for over a thousand years." He checked his watch. "But it's imperative that you listen carefully to what I'm about to say, because I don't have much longer; these intergalactic pneumatic holographic mail courier shaman services charge an arm and a leg. Really, it's murder. My point is this, Willy: waterslides. I want you to build a waterslide in my honor, or rather, our honor, and not just any old waterslide, no. It needs to be the tallest and loopiest waterslide in the history of waterslides! Simple as that. Don't overthink this. If you build it, they will come. You ever see that flick, Willy? Probably not. Rent it sometime. I love you, son, for all of eternity, and I'm sorry I quoted *Field of Dreams* just now."

And then Bruce Lee stopped spinning and my father vanished.

My mind went blank. My brain was broken, or so overloaded it just turned off. I had no thoughts at all, and no feelings, good or bad. I was blank. It was refreshing. I was untethered, free from all my problems and my parents' problems and the entire world's problems. Paroled for good behavior. For the first time in my life, my twenty-four-hours-a-day, seven-days-a-week, fifty-two-weeks-a-year internal dialogue that never stops stopped. Peace and quiet ensued, and it was paradise. I had momentarily transcended individuality, my body reduced to a rental car left at the airport, my ego dissolved like an Alka-Seltzer into the plasma river of infinity. In other words, my DNA was blowing naked in the wind, I had become one with the universe. Buddhists and grunge rock fanatics call this Nirvana, extinguishment of the fires that cause suffering: attachment, aversion, and ignorance.

The forest was teeming with crickets and coyotes and caterpillars and caribou. A great horned owl hooted, a chunky-cheeked chipmunk hollered. The night sky was alive with twinkling stars. The moon, no longer red, had returned to a more professional pale shade of yellow.

I was ready for bed. Bruce was still too dizzy to safely waddle home, so I had to carry him. We didn't talk. There were no words.

18

Despite the warm weather and lack of holiday decorations, it felt like Christmas morning when I woke up. I was snug in my bed but giddy with an unexplainable enthusiasm for something, though for the life of me, I could not remember what. I had never been so wide-eyed and supercharged so early in the morning. I checked my pulse and forehead to make sure I wasn't coming down with something, and then it hit me: I was ravenous. I desperately craved a toasted Cherry Pop-Tart with melted butter and an ice-cold glass of chocolate milk to wash it down. I rushed to the kitchen.

Extra, extra, read all about it. As luck would have it, Bumpkinville's illustrious mayor, Ron McDonald (no relation to the restaurant, he claims), was forced to pack his bags last night and move out of the mayoral double-wide trailer on Main Street after resigning his position, effective immediately, because of what was described in the *Bumpkinville Gazette* as "an illicit love triangle between the Mayor and Town Councilwoman Linda Fry and her twin sister, Town Controller Lucille O'Hapimeel."

My heart was skipping like a schoolgirl's at a Double Dutch competition as my mom read me the story. This was good news, great news, the best news I could ever have hoped for, as close to divine intervention as you get! The paper also reported that a special election for the new mayor would take place in ninety days. "Until then Town Council member and public school teacher Bob Dobalina will take over as Mayor."

Mr. Dobalina? Mr. Bob Dobalina is taking over as the temporary Mayor. What are the chances? I knew he didn't want the job, he'd said so over and over despite my repeated urgings, so he wouldn't stand in my way. In fact, he'd pave it for me, like Moses parting the Red Sea for the Israelites, in this case me. "Well, snap, crackle, and pop," I said as my mom tossed the paper aside. Things were looking up. "I'm going to run for mayor, Mom."

"What?"

"I want to be mayor of Bumpkinville, simple as that, and I need your support, if only as a registered voter."

"Why?" my mom demanded.

"So I'll win the election. It takes votes."

"No, why do you want to be mayor? What's gotten into you, sweetie pie?"

Just then Bruce Lee waddled into the kitchen like he was James

Brown, light on his feet but with so much swagger. He was disheveled, as much as a turtle can be.

"Good morning, sleepyhead," I said.

"You're looking awfully chipper this morning," he said. "What's gotten into you?"

"You're not going to believe what happened."

"Can you pour me some coffee?"

"We're out of the Peruvian stuff, sorry. But guess what."

"What?"

"The mayor of Bumpkinville has resigned!"

"And why did he do that?"

"Because of some McDonald's triangle fiasco or something. I'm not exactly sure. But we have hazelnut creamer."

"I love hazelnuts. So the mayor has resigned. How convenient."

The toaster bell rang. My mom popped my Pop-Tart onto my plate and spread some butter on it. While it melted I prepared some instant coffee with hazelnut creamer for Bruce. My mom seemed a little freaked out by this.

"Since when did you start drinking coffee?" she asked.

"It's for Bruce." I said, setting the coffee cup on the floor for Bruce to sip.

"You think all that caffeine and cream is good for a turtle?"

"I don't know, Mom, but he's like a hundred and fifty years old, so I'm gonna let him decide."

"Is that true?"

"Mm-hmm."

"I'm late for work. I'll see you tonight for dinner. Be good, sweetie pie."

"I'd love it if you didn't call me that."

"What?"

"Sweetie pie."

"Why?"

"Because it undermines my authority. You'll want me on your good side, Mom, trust me, so when I become mayor I don't have you audited or extradited."

"I should hope not," she said as she flew out the door.

"Bruce, was it a dream, or were you struck by lightning last night?"

"It's all a dream."

"So you were struck by lightning? Or you weren't?"

"I was."

"Why didn't it kill you?"

"My shell is magic, and it's made from a non-conducting material."

"Do you remember projecting a holographic message out of your eyeballs?"

"How could I possibly forget."

"It was the craziest thing I've ever seen, Bruce! Seriously, out-of-this-world insanity. I woke up this morning feeling like it was a dream or some bad cartoon I'd fallen asleep watching. Obviously, I can never tell anyone about this, maybe Daffodil, but that's it. Otherwise they might lock me up in the klink and throw away the key."

"Yeah, I'd probably keep this between us, at least until the election."

"Bruce, I feel like my life has purpose again, real meaning and closure, sort of. Don't get me wrong, I've been getting along just fine without any fatherly advice for more than half of my life at this point, but now my dad appears all of the sudden with a cryptic message expressing his dying wishes. He said he never fulfilled his life's dream because he was too busy trying to fulfill his father's dream and that I, in turn, should do the same thing. This seems like a conundrum---or is it a paradox?---and yet there's a certain grandeur to the idea of the world's tallest, loopiest waterslide ever, plus my dad didn't know about his dream until after he died, and now he's given it to me, and I'm still alive, and maybe his dream can be mine too. Why not? I'm curious, Bruce, what do you know about waterslides?"

"They're fun, I like them."

"Me too," I said, suddenly remembering that we had ridden on Dr. Von Dark's Tunnel of Terror together the summer before he died.

"But speaking of the election," Bruce said, "don't forget about your bet with Daffodil. You're going to need some more time preparing with me when you run for mayor, particularly if you win, and I have a strange feeling that today might be the day I go for broke." He spoke in no uncertain terms, wiping a dribble of coffee from his chin.

"It's too soon," I objected. "You're not ready. No man's ever done it this fast."

"I'm no man, Willy. I'm ready. I can feel it in my claws, they're itching to break free."

"It would be a miracle, Bruce. You'd be the first turtle in recorded history to have mastered the ancient art of Kung Fu---not counting the Teenage Mutant Ninja Turtles, but I'm told they have stunt doubles. If you're right, though, you'll be a hero and could probably make a lot of money out of it."

"I have no need for money," Bruce pointed out.

"That's true," I realized after giving it some thought. "But I do."

"What for?"

"If I had some money I could make an honest attempt at running for mayor. I need the money to buy votes."

Bruce gave a wry chuckle. "No, you just need ideas that will inspire people to vote for you. Don't focus on the money, Willy, focus on the seeds, and then the flowers will blossom and the money will follow."

"That's very poetic, Bruce, but I'm not growing a garden."

"Focus your energy on becoming the best mayor humanly possible. That's all you can do."

"Okay, fine," I said, "let's go."

I dragged Bruce and a two-by-four in my Radio Flyer up and over and down to the Penny Graveyard. As we rounded the last knoll, a sliver of sunlight broke through an otherwise cloudy and overcast day.

"Let's do some yoga, and then we can spar for a little while, and then we'll see what happens," Bruce said.

Two and a half hours later Bruce slammed his left claw into the two-by-four, splintering it to its core and severing it into two halves, like Romeo and Juliet, never to be reunited again. It was spectacular. A monumental achievement for reptiles everywhere.

It also brought me a deep sense of satisfaction to know that this was an indisputable display of karate ability by anyone's standards. I had done it, or Bruce had done it, but I had helped. If YouTube ever got hold of this he'd be famous, like a Beatle or *the Monkees*. He could never go to Disneyland or out in public again. I couldn't wait to see Daffodil. For one thing, I had won the bet, as she would soon see. For another, she wasn't going to believe everything that had happened over spring break. What a vacation. We had so much to catch up on. I just hoped she hadn't had a boring, uneventful week walking the plank.

19

"I can't speak for all of you, but that sure felt like the longest spring break of my life." Mr. Dobalina, drenched in sunlight, took a moment to gaze out the window longingly. "Goes to show you that everything, especially time, kids, is only relative. Somehow in one week I was able to complete a novella about a blind man living in a small New England fishing village going through a bitter divorce while overcoming mercury poisoning, and a one-act play about the unexpected pleasures of recycling. I also attended an emergency Town Council meeting, temporarily taking over as mayor, and I still had time to grade a few papers. Crazy, right?"

I shook my head in awe. Wow. He really was the coolest guy in the universe, and I hoped he knew it. He turned his back to the class and scribbled three important words onto the chalkboard, Capitalism, Socialism, and Communism. Then he turned around and said, "Before I begin, I guess I should ask if anyone is desperate to share a spring break highlight with the class."

I considered the various reactions I might receive if I divulged details about my holographic dad. Daffodil raised her hand, saving me from myself.

"Daffodil?" Mr. Dobalina said.

She stood up from her chair. She looked taller than I remembered, more sophisticated, worldly. She had a certain je ne sais quoi about her.

"A few years ago my grandfather acquired a very old treasure map on eBay," she said. "Flash forward in time to last week, the first day of spring break, and my dad and I fly down to Turks and Caicos in our seaplane to go looking for the treasure during my breaks from pirate camp, and guess what, we found it. It was really me who killed the sea monsters and actually discovered the treasure, but I couldn't have done it without my dad, he was instrumental. I'm just happy to be alive."

The class seemed as curious as they were dubious.

"I narrowly avoided death on several occasions," Daffodil went on. "There were so many booby traps and killer octopuses to avoid and pirates to contend with that it got a little ridiculous at times, but I persevered. Because that's what it takes."

Having yet to speak with Daffodil since her return, I was slightly incredulous. Her outlandish tales of heroism were rather farfetched, even by my standards, and from what I knew about octopuses, they weren't killers. Truth might be stranger than fiction, but still.

"Pirates?" I blurted out. "Seriously?"

Before Daffodil could respond, Mr. Dobalina interjected with a good question of his own. "Daffodil, I hate to pry, but are you at liberty to share with the class the total value of the treasure you managed to recover?"

"Around eight hundred million, give or take," she said.

My pulse quickened as she continued.

"There are so many jewels and bars of gold it'll probably take a while to get everything fully appraised, but it's somewhere in the eight-hundred-million-to-a-billion ballpark, I'd say. Of course, it will all go to charity."

"All of it?" I blurted again, like I had a sudden case of Tourette's.

"One hundred percent."

My heart sank into the sea like a treasure chest without a map. Did she really say that? Charity? All of it? Couldn't she keep just a little bit? The poor didn't need it all. They were used to having nothing. Plus, a few hundred million in my pocket could do so much good.

Mr. Dobalina led the class in a slow clap of appreciation for Daffodil, like at the end of the classic coming-of-age story *Lucas,* where Corey Haim's character returns from the hospital and Charlie Sheen and the rest of the football team jocks surprise him with his very own, three-sizes-too-big varsity letter jacket, simultaneously validating his entire existence and poking fun at his shrimpy stature. I assumed that in this case the class was clapping for Daffodil's selfless dedication to humanity, specifically those less fortunate than her, which I'm pretty sure was everyone, and Daffodil definitely deserved a slow clap if Corey Haim did. She was a modern-day preteen Mother Teresa who would make for one heck of an adviser to the mayor when the time came.

"Thank you, Daffodil," Mr. Dobalina said as she sat down. "Okay, class," he declared, "today we're going to learn about Capitalism and Socialism and Communism. Does anyone know what these words mean?"

I raised my hand with a flourish. I was all over this one.

"Yes, Willy?"

"I happen to know a few things about politics, Mr. Dobalina. Remember how you always joked that I should run for mayor one day? Well, surprise, surprise, I've decided to do it."

"But Willy, as you pointed out so astutely, I was only joking."

"I know, but what the heck, right? I happen to have learned a thing or two about laissez-faire capitalism and interventionism and the general concept of socialism. I listened to *The Communist Manifesto* on Audible.com, in an inspired reading by Wesley Snipes, so I'd like to take this opportunity to present a rough sketch of what my policies will be so you know exactly where I'm coming from."

Mr. Dobalina seemed uncharacteristically stunned, but he kindly obliged my request to explain my political platform. "Go ahead, Willy, the floor's yours."

I took center stage before the chalkboard. "First, I'd like to thank you all for being here. As the future mayor of Bumpkinville I have three major initiatives I'd like to focus on today. Please don't be alarmed if anything I say sounds too extreme or communistic, trust me, it's not. Number one is education reform. First thing we do is fire all schoolteachers, yep, every last one. Sorry, Mr. Dobalina. What's fair is fair."

Not one to take things personally, Mr. Dobalina nodded approvingly.

"Through a rigorous selection process, we choose the seven smartest teachers in the world, and their job is to teach the subjects that we determine to be the ideal curriculum. Then Steven Spielberg, ideally, films them every day in a Hollywood sound stage while they lecture to a studio audience, and then the lectures are broadcast to every classroom in the country. For the first time in recorded history, regardless of socioeconomic background or geographic location, every school kid in America will be ensured a world-class education. The best part is that taxpayers will save hundreds of billions in teacher salaries every year! It's a win-win. We cut the education budget but get a better education! My number two initiative is space exploration. I want to reignite the space race, like Kennedy did, by making it a top priority for every man, woman, and child to have their own rocket ship, either leased or owned outright, by the end of the decade. This might sound superfluous, but once we develop a Disney Moon Theme Park and some discount shopping outlets, it'll all start to make sense. Not to mention all the jobs it will create. And finally, number three, my defense plan, the most important of all. Here goes: we completely eliminate the military, all of it, everything, gone! Except, of course, for the special elite secret forces that other countries don't know much about. We also get rid of all our nuclear weapons. Except, of course, for a handful that we hide in a mountain somewhere in Colorado or Idaho, just to be safe."

"That's a very interesting political landscape you've painted for us, Willy, but perhaps it's more appropriate for the president of the United States, say, than the mayor of Bumpkinville?" Mr. Dobalina inquired.

"I agree one hundred percent, that's exactly where this train ends up, but let's not get ahead of ourselves, Mr. Dobalina, one step at a time. I don't want to bite off more than I can chew, as the old expression goes," I said, and then kept on jabbering. "By eliminating the armed forces completely, Americans will save over one trillion dollars a year, maybe more. And I propose that we spend a majority of that savings to produce better television shows. Now hear me out, just imagine for a second what would happen if TV shows became totally compelling, with nail-biting suspense and heart-wrenching drama and beautifully flawed characters in original story lines with unexpected twists. I believe irritable and potentially hostile countries would cooperate with us rather than risk their favorite shows being canceled prematurely. I call this preemptive entertainment. I'm hoping to win the Nobel for this. When the time comes."

Silence. Nobody spoke. There was only heavy breathing until Mr. Dobalina said, "Class, if not our votes, I think we owe Willy a round of applause for his uniquely post-Marxist, neo-dictatorial, multitopian vision for Bumpkinville. I'd say he's got a bright future ahead."

Daffodil clapped a couple of times, but that was all. Well, Legoland wasn't built in a day, I consoled myself.

I sat down and slouched low in my chair and listened to Mr. Dobalina explain the difference between capitalism and communism, which he boiled down to being about the individual versus the collective. He explained that communism was a variation on socialism in essence, and that socialism was a reaction to capitalism, which was a reaction to totalitarianism or monarchy, which themselves were simply a reaction to barbarism, back in the very beginning.

"Does anyone know what barbarism is? And no, Willy, it has nothing to do with getting a haircut, but it has everything to do with cutting our hair, as a species, in an evolutionary sense. Does that make sense?"

"Is that a paradox?" I asked.

"No," Mr. Dobalina said. "It's not."

20

Everyone's favorite feminine swashbuckler and I had a chance to catch up during recess. We rode on opposing polyethylene spring-loaded playground animals, a yellow and purple parrot for the lady, a classic green crocodile for me.

"Since when," I said in disbelief, "did octopuses become killers?"

"When a hundred-and-fifty-pound venomous cephalopod is attacking you, it's kill or be killed. That's just the way it is."

"I guess that makes you a hero."

"I guess."
"And it's all going to charity?"
"Yep."
"You're sure?"
"Uh-huh."
"What a waste."
"The Red Cross can do a lot with the loot."
"They've been dogged by controversies for years. "
"I didn't know that," Daffodil said, almost raising an eyebrow.
"They're more corrupt than the Indian government, at least according to the Hong Kong-based group Political and Economic Risk Consultancy, which surveyed more than thirteen hundred business executives in twelve Asian countries."
"About the Red Cross?"
"No, the Indian government."
"What are you saying?"
"That a small contribution to the Willy Nilly Charity Foundation for a Better Tomorrow will make a lot of people happy. Starting right here." I pointed at myself.
"And what exactly is this charity of yours all about?"
"Well, to be honest, it's fairly new, we're not technically a 501(3) organization quite yet, which means there's time for a high-level collaboration. The clay isn't dry, we can still mold our charity into whatever we want if we work together. Hand in hand."
"But what are the core tenets, what's the point?"

"All I know for sure is that my foundation is committed to building low-cost, high-style homeless condominiums, just like you, and to financing my mayoral campaign. And a waterslide."

"A waterslide? Why?"

"You want the truth?"

"Of course."

"Bruce Lee and I performed a shamanic ceremony the other day and managed to conjure my dad from the dead in the form of a cryptic holographic message."

"Of course you did," she said, blatantly mocking me.

"No, really. No kidding. Cross my heart and hope to die."

"Not that I believe you, but what did he say?"

"He professed his love for waterslides. He said that the Nilly family name and the fate of his restless soul hinged on my unwavering dedication to building him a waterslide."

"Why, as an homage? I don't get it."

"Yeah, sort of. He said it was all up to me to fulfill his dying dream. Which is nerve-racking, I admit, but a healthy challenge. Now my life has purpose."

"To build a waterslide for your dad?"

"Not just any old waterslide, the biggest and slipperiest waterslide in the world, a symbol of individuality and personal freedom plus the collective power of collaboration, with more twists and turns and unexpected dips and drops and flips and flops than life itself. Trust me, it will blow your mind. People will travel from all over the world to ride on it. The Great Wall of China, the Taj Mahal, Petra, Mecca, Disneyland, none of them will hold a candle to Bumpkinville when I'm done with this place. I'm talking Eighth Wonder of the World here."

"Then why are you wasting your time running for mayor if all you want to do is build a waterslide?"

Daffodil's astuteness was bewitching. "The waterslide is only one piece of the puzzle. As mayor I plan to introduce the waterslide program as the key initiative in rejuvenating the town's taxable tourism revenue and creating new jobs along with a renewed sense of pride---the triple bottom line. Additionally, like you, I want to eradicate homelessness once and for all, and I need your help, Daffodil."

The recess bell rang. We stopped boinking.

Daffodil turned and stared deeply into my soul. "Do you want to come over after school and float around in my zero-gravity chamber? It's fun and it's finally fixed."

Lost in her gaze, I nodded. I most definitely did. We dismounted the parrot and crocodile, respectively, and headed back to class.

21

I took Bruce Lee and a two-by-four to Daffodil's with me. She was overjoyed to see him, and overwhelmed by his karate prowess.

"I should never have doubted you about your dad, Willy. If Bruce can chop blocks, he can do anything," she said as we returned him to his life in the lap of his luxury aquarium."

There was no denying our camaraderie. It was palpable. Daffodil and I had so much in common. She lived life adventurously, she laughed at my jokes occasionally, and we shared custody of a turtle. Weightlessness adds a certain ethereal quality to any conversation, sure, but still, our rapport was effortless, as if we were long-lost friends. If the world was our oyster, then hanging out in a zero-gravity chamber was the pearl.

"I was forced to walk the plank," she said, floating upside down, "with knives at my throat. That's when I had the most vivid yet surreal sensation of stepping outside of my body and my individuality altogether. I was actually watching what was happening to me as if it wasn't me at all. It was so peculiar that I completely stopped being afraid of the drunken pirates and watched with amusement as they forced me into the savage sea. And it's because I kept my wits about me and didn't panic that I'm still alive."

"How did you survive?"

"A dolphin rescued me. She hooked her nose through the rope tied around my wrists and dragged me to the nearest deserted island, which happened to be in the vicinity of where Blackbeard's treasure was buried. As luck would have it."

"They call what you had on the plank an out-of-body experience. I've done a little research. The concept of disembodied consciousness is nothing new, it's as old as time, yet rarely is it discussed in polite company, regrettably."

"I find etiquette so inappropriate most of the time."

"It's archaic, really. If you think about it."

"Grotesque, even."

"The way I see it, Daffodil, is the way I first saw it back when we were toasting with your raspberry tears. Your altruism combined with my serious commitment to fun would be the perfect formula."

"Formula for what?"

"For political power. Look, the Willy Nilly Charity Foundation for a

Better Tomorrow needs a seventeen-thousand-dollar tax-deductible contribution by Monday so we can hire a professional political marketing company to blanket Bumpkinville with pro-Willy Nilly propaganda. I'm counting on it to get me elected."

"Sounds like a long shot."

"Along with my press conference introducing my new political party, and a few radio plugs, I think there's a chance."

"I like your confidence, but what's in it for me?"

"If I'm mayor, that makes you the trusted adviser to the mayor. You'll have my ear, you'll be my right hand, my chief of staff, the big cheese, the brains behind the organization. I'm just a kid who's good with a teleprompter, but it's your show, I'm just your warm-up act. You'll write all the speeches and I'll be your puppet, I just want the attention and power. And if it all goes as planned, I should rocket from mayor to governor to president before we're old enough to rent a car."

"You have to be thirty-five to be president."

"Then I'll have that law changed."

"How?"

"I'll pay lobbyists and bribe congressmen."

"So you know what you're doing?"

"Sort of."

"And you think money is the solution."

"No, empathy is the solution, which you have in spades, Daffodil. Throw in a pragmatist like myself and just a little bit of money and there's no telling what's possible."

"I think you might have what it takes to go all the way, Willy Nilly."

"All the way to where?"

"Wherever you want."

I took a moment to fully absorb the magnitude of that statement. It was off the Richter scale. "That's the nicest thing anyone's ever said to me."

"You're welcome."

"Thank you."

"I'll do it."

"Do what?"

"Be your partner, contribute to your charity, why not. We can change the world together," Daffodil said, giving herself a little push, and we floated together quietly and companionably until it was time to go home.

In the morning, after the interminable bus ride to school, I went looking for Mr. Dobalina. As I suspected, I found him in the teachers' lounge.

"Mr. Dobalina, I need your support," I said.

"You have it, Willy. You know that."

"No, I mean publicly, for mayor. I need your endorsement. My political consultants tell me that without it my chances are slim, at best."

"But you know I can't do that, Willy. I'm running for mayor too."

"You are? You could have mentioned that sooner. I thought you were just the acting mayor until the election."

"No," Mr. Dobalina said, uncharacteristically failing to elaborate.

"Okay, fine, but do you really need to be mayor, Mr. Dobalina, on top of everything else? Can't you throw me a bone?"

"Willy, I like your passion and your unconventional perspective, but I don't think the good people of Bumpkinville are progressive enough to elect a ten-year-old mayor. This is a town beset by conundrums and paradoxes, and you still don't know the meaning of those words."

"Paradox-shmaradox. I resent ageism, whether casual or systemic, and I'm surprised you can look the other way."

"Ageism usually means discrimination toward seniors, Willy. Old people, not kids."

"Have you ever heard of Brian Zimmerman? He was only eleven years old when he was elected mayor of Crabb, Texas. So there."

"I wish you all the luck in the world, Willy."

"I don't believe in luck anymore."

"Why not?"

"It's a long story, I'll tell you some other time. As the current acting mayor, can you at least expedite a temporary beverage permit for me so I can serve refreshments at my press conference?"

"I'll see what I can do."

"Thank you. And Mr. Dobalina, either way, no hard feelings, right?"

"Right."

It had never occurred to me that I'd be running against any formidable opponents, much less Mr. Dobalina. I thought the mayoral seat was wide open and all I'd have to do was swoop in with the altruism/fun combo and that would be that. Sighing, I trudged off to my first class, English---we were reading *Richard III*, appropriately. Somehow I made it through the rest of the tedious and torturous day, buoyed, no doubt, by Daffodil's unwavering confidence in me.

At home that night, I called a family meeting. It was time to spill the beans. We gathered in the living room and sipped hot chocolate with little marshmallows and watched *Jeopardy* on TV, an unspoken family tradition. For the first time ever, I wasn't able to correctly question any of Alex Trebek's answers, not a single one.

"Mom, Tunafish, I'm glad you're both sitting down," I said during the first commercial break, "because I have some very exciting news to share with you. I'm about to launch my first political campaign to become Bumpkinville's next mayor, and the youngest in American history. Inevitably the press and the pundits will heavily scrutinize us, it could get pretty ugly, so I need you to be prepared. But I want you to know that when the dust settles it'll be worth it, and I'd appreciate your support, especially since you're both old enough to vote. A small contribution wouldn't hurt either."

Total silence, except for the *Jeopardy* theme music, which perfectly accented the moment. I could see my mom searching for the right words, and then they came to her.

"Willy, have you lost your mind?"

"No, of course not, where would it have gone?"

"And this isn't a practical joke?"

"Nope."

"I thought you were joking when you mentioned it the other day."

"I wasn't. Listen, it's not uncommon, Mom, to be skeptical when extraordinary news like this presents itself. I can relate, I've gone through a few moments of disbelief myself, but trust me when I tell you this is no joke."

"Running for mayor, Willy Nilly, is completely out of the question. Do you hear me? I do not want you to run for mayor under any circumstance. Got it?"

"Mom, this is my true calling, the reason I was put here on Planet Earth, and you want to stand in my way. How could you?"

"Since when did politics become so important to you?" she demanded.

"Since recently," I said, "and I don't appreciate your harsh knee-jerk reaction."

"I'd like to hear some details about your political aspirations," my mom said.

"You probably just ate too much candy," Uncle Tunafish chimed in.

"I'll be holding a press conference tomorrow to explain my brand-new political party," I said. "And I could use a ride."

22

The night before the press conference I couldn't sleep. Not a wink. My mind was adrift, lost at sea, sunburned and dehydrated and hopeless. As the sharks circled, I tossed and turned, my thoughts like schooners sailing directly into gale-force winds. I tried to imagine pleasant things, happy things, like kitty cats and bunny rabbits, or what it would feel like being the first ruler of Planet Earth, with unilateral control, always on the go, yet still able to mix business and pleasure while governing with the easy touch of an iPad mini from the plush leather seats and unbeatable views of a Gulfstream V. The business card alone! Still, I couldn't stay focused. There was an irritating family of babushka dolls illegally squatting in my head and endlessly opening inward upon themselves, getting smaller and smaller but never disappearing, until the maddening repetition was just too much.

It was still dark. The moon was lemon-lime green and casting a sickly hospital-room tint on the world. I was a nervous wreck. I ate a frosted cherry Pop-Tart and tried to meditate, but that didn't help, so I showered and put on my favorite Walter Mondale for President tee shirt, which never fails to put a smile on my face. I moussed my hair, slipped on some socks and my lucky green corduroys, Velcroed my sneakers tight, and tied my navy cardigan sweater around my waist, in case it got chilly later, and to project an image of responsibility. From what I could tell, I looked smart and dependable, like someone you could trust and maybe even vote for. The roosters still hadn't cock-a-doodle-dooed after all that, so I sat down to read the last few chapters of *Nixonland: The Rise of a President and the Fracturing of America*.

After what seemed like several weeks later, the sun finally came up and the chickens laid their eggs and my mom prepared her famous gluten-free banana and blueberry pancakes, especially for me, with a side of burned bacon and a glass of orange juice.

Then, cementing her nomination for the Greatest Mom in the World Award, she drove me to town. Tunafish was too busy sleeping, of course--- it's surprising he's not better looking.

My mom asked if I had prepared a speech.

"Sort of," I told her. "I'd like it to feel off the cuff, in a free-flowing stream-of-consciousness kind of way, if you know what I mean, but I don't want to forget any important parts either. It's a tightrope walk."

It was 9:42 a.m. when we stopped for a parade of cows, hundreds of thousands of them, maybe millions, leisurely crossing the street. This concerned me considerably. If I was late to my own press conference, then what? My pulse quickened. I loosened my collar and wiped my forehead. Don't panic, I told myself. Breathe.

At 9:57 a.m., when we arrived, I was in a full panic. A temporary platform and podium had been erected for my presentation in the center of Town Square. It looked pretty good. There was a small crowd, not huge, but nothing to shake a stick at either, and if things didn't go well there was no chance of being trampled to death by a mob of frenzied voters.

Daffodil, wearing a giant *Vote Willy Nilly* button on her blouse, was serving raspberry teardrops to passersby. I waved to her and she smiled reassuringly. There were at least a dozen adoring---or if not adoring, then placid, bordering on pleasant---townspeople standing around, staring at me, waiting, I guess, for me to take the stage.

Mr. Dobalina was there too, off to the side, casually leaning against a big oak tree sipping teardrops and smoking a bubble pipe. Mosquito and Tilo were blowing bubbles front and center. My least favorite vice-principal was there, Mr. Shmutz, no doubt to scrutinize me. What a bastard. And who else was there? None other than the deputy-doofus, anti-lemonade, swat-team policeman himself. He was still wearing a spandex onesie, a silly hat, and a lame #2 pencil-thin mustache, but this time around, he was assigned to protect me and keep the crowd orderly for my permit-approved---thanks in large part to Mr. Dobalina---event. I couldn't help but appreciate this ironic reversal of fortune.

Just before I took the stage Mr. Policeman turned to me and said, "See, kid, there is justice in the world, you just have to follow the rules or we're no better than apes."

I contemplated that for a moment. I disagreed, but I nodded anyway. I hopped up to the stage and grabbed the microphone tenderly, like Elvis might have.

"Ladies and gentlemen, first I'd like to thank you all for coming out on such a beautiful day to hear my vision for Bumpkinville's future. Second, I'd like to thank my friend Daffodil for serving her secret-recipe raspberry drink on behalf of the Willy Nilly Betterment of America campaign, and for pledging a part of Blackbeard's treasure, which she discovered over spring break---I'm sure you all read about it in the *Gazette*---to abolishing homelessness by building state-of-the-art condos to house those without houses. Next I'd like to thank my mom for driving me here this morning, and finally I'd like to thank the town, particularly Mr. Bob Dobalina, for permitting me the opportunity to present my brand-new and potentially revolutionary political ideas to you all." I took a long pause to build anticipation. Mosquito and Tilo even stopped blowing bubbles.

"It's my dream that one day soon Republicans and Democrats alike will be nothing more than a historical diorama in Bumpkinville's Museum of Natural History, a relic of the past, a foul, unpleasant memory from the nineteenth and twentieth centuries of what didn't work for America. This isn't football, people, we're not playing hockey, this isn't a competition against ourselves, it's the opposite, it's a competition to see who can work together the best, so let's stop the mud wrestling and come together as one. With no further ado, I proudly present my new political party. Ladies and gentlemen, the Preposterous Party. Ta-da!"

Daffodil popped a cork from a fresh bottle of raspberry teardrops at precisely the right moment. What a girl.

I didn't expect mass hysteria, but I did expect something. There was no visible or audible response from anyone in the audience, not to say that there wasn't a response, just not a visible or an audible one. They were probably shocked.

"Okay, people, don't everyone all freak out at once," I joked. "I know this is very exciting, and maybe even a little bit overwhelming for some of you, so let me first try and explain the core philosophies behind the new party as simply as I can. You see, the Preposterous Party believes, basically, that everyone's approach to everything in life is entirely wrong, and that only by intentionally being preposterous all the time will we ever accomplish anything truly great."

Mosquito and Tilo seemed utterly perplexed. I kept going.

"Only by seeing the world preposterously does it cease to be preposterous, and may in fact, in some cases, actually start to make sense. If you think about it, you'll see what I mean, but instead of boring you all to death with the details, I'll cut to the chase, attractive and talented townspeople that you are: if you decide to vote for me, Willy Nilly, as your next mayor of Bumpkinville, I promise to use your hard-earned taxpayer dollars to build the largest and most spectacular waterslide on Planet Earth. Take a breath, I know it's staggering, almost too good to be true---finally a politician who gets it, right? This waterslide will drive tourism like no other, and bring jobs back and revitalize the entire town, but that's not why I ask for your vote, no. Townspeople, as I look down upon you today, I know that I will be a good ruler to you all, and if you kindly offer me your vote, in return I will offer you my heart and soul and brain on a silver platter."

I let the extreme silence that had prevailed throughout the speech punctuate the moment.

"And if I'm elected, as an extra special bonus, as if I were a late-night TV pitchman selling indestructible steak knives, but instead I'm selling important political initiatives, I will establish the Bumpkinville Aeronautics and Space Administration, or BASA for short, which is a top priority of mine. Folks, I'm proposing we start this yesterday. Time is of the essence, because the federal government, speaking candidly, isn't pulling their weight in this department. In conclusion, I beg you all to please vote for me, Willy Nilly."

Then, for my grand finale, I yanked out my favorite yellow and black Duncan Bumblebee yo-yo and performed a near perfect Daring Young Man on the Flying Trapeze for a crowd of captivated voters. "Thank you for coming, and thank you, William Saroyan. Long live Bumpkinville."

The townspeople seemed slightly bemused, but I was a hero in my mind. I had hit my talking points, I had delivered my message. Evel Knievel probably never felt this good after breaking hundreds of bones. I was on top of the world, master of the universe, capable of anything, loved by all. I was a legend in the making.

A CNN reporter was the first to ask if I was serious about all this, and "why a waterslide?"

"Yes, I'm serious, like a pop quiz is. And it's important to understand that the waterslide, although a seemingly silly and arbitrary concept, is actually an ingenious, if I do say so myself, attempt to stimulate a depressed economy, bringing hope and prosperity and maybe even some pride back to the people." I should have stopped talking right then, at that moment---less is more, remember that---because the next part was the clip they used on the news. "This is not some seat-of-my-pants, fly-by-night, flimflam operation, no sirree Bob."

A snarky reporter asked, "Who's Bob?"

"Bob is a figure of speech," I said. "This is the Preposterous Party, people! And you're all invited. Are there any more questions?"

A sinister Fox News reporter asked me, "Are you intentionally mocking democracy, or is it accidental?"

"Of course it's intentional," I said. "I have to mock it. It's my job. What choice do I have as president of the Preposterous Party? It's my responsibility, my obligation, and my sincere pleasure. Don't get me wrong, I earnestly want to be mayor of Bumpkinville so I can inject a much-needed breath of fresh air into an otherwise scandalized and corrupt system. And selfishly, I admit, since you're asking, it can't hurt on my college admissions."

I shared a funny little moment with my new policeman friend as I stepped off the stage; he nodded his head slightly, respectfully tipping his cap down and right back up as fast as possible, so no one else would notice, I assumed. But I noticed. It was subtle, old-fashioned, almost imperceptible, but significant just the same---an indication, perhaps, of what was to come now that I was a politician.

I noticed a penny glimmering in the grass, like in the good old days. I walked over and picked it up. I closed my eyes and thought about my dad and his waterslide and my political future, and like the champion wish maker I once was, I wished that I was mayor of Bumpkinville! Presto, like a judge's gavel slamming down, it was a mere formality now. I had made my wish and it was all but guaranteed to come true this time.

When I opened my eyes I felt like a giant newborn baby ready to float away, my sense of optimism completely renewed. The possibilities were limitless. I couldn't help but feel like I had accomplished something extraordinary. I had boldly thrown a wrench into the hypocritical political system of Bumpkinville. My crusade to invert the world's hierarchy without creating total anarchy was officially underway. I had catapulted from oppressed to oppressor, and it felt good. I was on my way.

There was two weeks to go before the election. I spent all my free time after school buttonholing townspeople, promoting, pleading, promising. When Election Day finally came I lost by a landslide. It was nearly unanimous against me, apparently, but I've demanded a recount, just to be sure. I don't see the town jumping on that request anytime soon, but like I said, no hard feelings, because Mr. Bob Dobalina, the one and only, was the winner, surprise surprise, and if he didn't deserve to be mayor, then I don't know who did. I'd have voted for him myself if I was old enough.

One day I'll be mayor and I'll build that damn waterslide too, and it'll be the next truly great architectural achievement since the pyramids, and my father will rest in peace, and Bumpkinville will thank me, not that I need thanks, no, but a little appreciation from time to time never hurts. I wouldn't refuse a little bronze statue in my likeness in Town Square, for instance, and I mean life-size, and why not make it platinum so it doesn't rust.

Epilogue

Papa Peacock piloted his six-million-dollar Dornier Seastar amphibious seaplane south, over Wyoming, Colorado, New Mexico, Mexico, Guatemala, Nicaragua, Costa Rica, Panama, Columbia, Ecuador, the west coast of Brazil (for a minute), and Peru. Daffodil and Willy and Bruce Lee nibbled cashews and mini-pretzels, sipped ginger ale, and played cutthroat pinochle the whole time. Bruce, in an unprecedented display of trickery, successfully shot the moon three times before the plane glided down, skimming gently across the surface of Lake Titicaca.

In a roofless hut on a floating island nearby, Miguel Battabooshka Guadeloupe Garcia-Rodriguez was brewing cappuccinos and roasting grasshoppers over a fire, eagerly anticipating his old and new friends' arrival.

Made in the USA
Middletown, DE
20 June 2015